MW00917478

SUNNY SIDE UP

A Deadline Cozy Mystery Book 1

SONIA PARIN

ISBN-10: 1537026755

ISBN-13: 978-1537026756

Chapter One

"I'M NOT BITING the bullet. I'm only taking a small nibble." Eve Lloyd pushed back her sunglasses and stared at the bridge separating the island from the mainland. Once she crossed it, there'd be no going back. She'd been thinking of nothing else for the past twelve months.

Talk about dragging her feet.

Twelve months of trying to find another solution and this was the best she could come up with...

Running away and hiding.

"It's only temporary," she told herself and put her car into gear.

The day her divorce had become final, her aunt Mira had put her arm around her and had urged her to come stay with her for however long it took to glue herself back together again. No conditions attached.

Eve bobbed her head from side to side, her glossy brown hair sliding along her shoulders.

On that day, she'd thought she'd never get over losing the man she'd assumed had been the love of her life. And while her aunt's house came with all the perks of comfortable living, Eve had wanted to keep moving. Actually, she hadn't had a choice in the matter. The restaurant she'd owned with her husband had needed a complete sink or swim makeover. It had been her way of moving on, her focus fixed on making a success of the business he'd ripped apart.

At the time, coming to stay on the island would have felt too much like coddling... wrapping herself up in cotton wool and turning a blind eye to everything she had to face. Besides, she simply hadn't been able to stop. Her instinct had pushed her to soldier on.

Now, however...

It had all finally caught up with her.

She was done with the restaurant business.

Time to start writing a new chapter...

She'd stay two weeks... maybe a month. Long enough to figure out what she wanted to do and get her life back on track. Besides, she owed her aunt a visit. And...

If worse came to worst, she might take her up on her long-standing offer to work for her. She could think of it as a working vacation, doing what, she had no idea. But it would at least be a solid block of thinking time, long enough to redefine herself and still have something to do.

Dismissing the stray thought, she reached for her phone and searched for her aunt's number, but instead of her aunt's cheerful voice she got the answering machine.

"Mira. I'm taking you up on your open invitation..." Eve ran the phrase through her mind and tried to think of what else she might add to the message. She'd last seen her aunt a year ago and before that...

She received regular updates on Mira's comings and goings. Her aunt had never learned the meaning of slowing down. In her early sixties, she spent the summer months alternating between cruising the Caribbean and Mediterranean, while winters were spent on the island working on her next bestseller. A romantic woman who lived by her own rules, Mira Lloyd, a.k.a. Elizabeth Lloyd, renowned author of sweltering historical romances, liked nothing better than to play matchmaker.

Just so long as she stuck to doing it on paper.

And if she didn't...

"I'll kill you, Mira." Her aunt had her ways and Eve didn't think she was up to standing up to her antics. She could be quite devious... but not insensitive, Eve reminded herself. Then again, she'd already dropped a hint... but she hadn't pursued it.

Your happiness will be your best revenge.

And in Mira's opinion, you couldn't have happiness without romance...

Eve had chosen her own brand of revenge. Resurrecting the restaurant from the ashes of her ex-husband's embezzlement.

She should have been savoring the sweetness. After all, she'd won. She'd survived. Yes, but...

Then she'd fizzled.

Throwing herself into survival mode had left her wrung out.

She straightened in her seat. "It's now or never." With a groan, Eve put away her phone and focused on the last leg of her trip.

She watched the sun making its descent toward the horizon. Her gaze skated over the bay and lingered over the gentle waves reflecting echoes of the last glimmers of the day. After her long drive, she wanted to settle in before nightfall. But she didn't want to arrive empty-handed.

Driving along the picturesque two-lane road leading to the town, she tried to remember what the little island had to offer.

If she could trust her memory, the Chin Wag Café excelled at pies and cakes, including their award winning blueberry extravaganza. Knowing her aunt favored the vegetable tarts and chocolate mousse cakes, she decided to make quick work of it and get some.

She pulled into the first available parking space and climbed out, taking a moment to stretch her legs and get her bearings. And that's when the feeling of having stepped into an alternative universe swamped her.

Everything moved at a different rhythm here.

A leisurely pace she could barely abide.

Everyone knew everyone.

With the summer season over, the weather had cooled down and the locals had the island to themselves again. She watched a family step out of a restaurant and stop for a chat with a young couple. A man driving by waved and called out a greeting to a woman sitting at a sidewalk café.

This was all so far removed from what she knew, living in the city, with its hectic pace, never seeing her neighbors, never even getting to learn their names because they never seemed to stand still long enough for her to find out. Not that she'd ever had the time to socialize...

"Are you lost?"

Eve smiled to herself. It had only taken a few minutes to be spotted and slotted as an outsider.

"No, I'm not. Thank you for asking." She looked at the man and tried to place the face. Sixty something, maybe pushing seventy, well dressed and, despite the terse look on one half of his face, he came across as friendly as he could be without appearing too suspicious of her. He lived in a house not far from her aunt's and had earned the distinction of being the best gardener on the island.

Eve hesitated. Growing up, she'd spent most of her summer holidays with her aunt. One year she'd—

Not wanting to wear her guilt on her face, Eve took a deep swallow and tried to shake off the memory of stealing the man's entire crop of roses to give to her aunt.

"Do I know you?" he asked.

"I'm..." She pasted on a confident smile, "I'm Eve Lloyd. Mira Lloyd's niece," she said and tried to recall the man's name. Harold? Harry?

"Henry Parkmore," he offered as if reading her mind. "We haven't seen you around in a while. How long's it been? Two years?" he asked, his tone carrying an accusatory edge.

"Just about."

Henry Parkmore appeared to be considering his next question. Not wanting to face the inevitable ones about her ex, she smiled and excused herself.

"Lovely to see you again, Mr. Parkmore. I'm afraid I have to rush off."

Crossing the street, she looked over her shoulder in time to see him stop a passer-by and point at her.

The fuse had been lit. It wouldn't take long for word to spread now.

When she stepped inside the Chin Wag Café, she made a point of avoiding eye contact with any of the customers and made a beeline for the counter. There'd be plenty of time to look around and reacquaint herself with some of the locals. Although, if she had her way, she'd spend her stay on the island sitting on a lounger with pen and paper. Somehow, she'd figure out what to do with the rest of her life. Even if the thought of having to start from scratch exhausted her.

"Can I help you?"

"Yes." She placed her order and, noticing a display of gourmet coffee and tea, she decided to splurge.

As she turned to leave, another local approached her.

"Eve?"

This time she had no trouble recognizing the man. She took in his distinguished Cary Grant good looks and bright blue eyes that always sparkled with a hint of mischief. "Patrick McKenzie."

He gave her a small smile. "You remember."

She returned the smile with an added chuckle. How could she forget the man who'd been pining after her aunt all these years? A retired history professor with a talent for storytelling, Eve had often wondered why her aunt had never taken to him. Now who was the matchmaker?

"Of course, I do. How are you?"

"Very well. I heard about—"

She raised a hand to stop him. "I appreciate the sentiment." But she was done hearing them.

"Yes, of course. Mira never mentioned you'd be coming. She often worries about leaving the house empty while she travels. I do the best I can to keep an eye on it. Good of you to come."

Eve frowned. "Is my aunt away?"

"Well... yes. You didn't know? She went on one of her trips. Said she had some serious thinking to do." He shook his head. "Your timing is unfortunate."

Strange, Eve thought. Her aunt always let her know before going on one of her trips. She struggled to hide her disappointment. Eve had wanted a quiet break away from it all, but she hadn't necessarily wanted to be alone.

Chapter Two

EVE DUG around her handbag for her set of house keys. Her chat with Patrick McKenzie had turned into a sit down catch up meal at the local pub. She hadn't been able to help herself and had rambled on about Alex, revealing everything there was to say about her embezzling ex and how wrung out she felt after throwing herself into the business of recovering her losses.

Hearing Patrick say the man should be flogged for putting her through such an ordeal had given her an unexpected feeling of relief and satisfaction. Alex had been... was a charmer and no one could ever find fault with him. In her opinion, he deserved more than a flogging.

"The man's a candidate for murder," Eve had said.

She smiled as she recalled Patrick chuckling. She'd

needed to let her hair down and have a free for all heart to heart.

Very liberating, she couldn't help thinking.

But as good as it had felt to finally open up about her grievances, now the sun had set and she had to navigate her way to the front veranda of her aunt's beach house in the dark.

Taking only her small suitcase, she decided to get the rest of her luggage in the morning. She made her way along the pebbled path regretting she hadn't arrived in time to see the pretty blue house in the light of day.

It always gave her a feeling of homecoming.

As a teenager, she'd spent her summer months here while her parents traveled overseas on business. They'd both been in their late thirties when she'd come along, a surprise package they hadn't counted on... or scheduled.

As busy corporate lawyers, they'd led a hyperactive lifestyle trotting around the world. Eve had attended a boarding school and at sixteen had run away for the first time. Long hours of counseling had straightened her out and she'd eventually pulled up her socks long enough to graduate; the least she could do for her parents after they'd invested in her future. However, regardless of how much effort she put into her life, she'd ended up making a career out of disappointing them.

She'd met her husband at a wine tasting show. Eve had been making her own way working for a catering company and still going through her self-discovery phase trying to find something that could hold her interest long enough for her to try to make a success of it. In the end, it had turned out to be marriage and a restaurant. She'd fallen hard for Alex and within a month had married him in a civil ceremony with only her aunt Mira to witness the then happy event.

To this day, her parents hadn't stopped being disappointed in the way she'd turned out, the food industry falling far below their standards. Her aunt, on the other hand, had always simply smiled, offering her support in whatever she did.

Eve pushed the front door open and searched for the light switch. As she stepped inside, the fresh smell of the ocean followed her in.

She made her way up the stairs to the bedroom that was always ready for her, the bed looking so inviting her knees wobbled and she almost collapsed onto it. Not yet, she thought.

At the foot of the bed, she noticed a couple of colorful quilts that hadn't been there the last time she'd visited, a sign her aunt had stuck to her plans to visit Amish country, something she'd meant to do for some time but had kept postponing in favor of one of her more exotic adventures.

Without thinking about it, she strode over to the window and drew the curtains open. It was always the first thing she did when she arrived. The house sat right on the beach. Day or night, she could look out the window and take in the pretty view.

A long bath later and with no catch-up chat to look forward to with her aunt, she settled in for the night with one of her aunt's romance books and promptly fell asleep. Sometime close to midnight, however, she stirred awake and remembered the pie and cake she'd left in the car.

Hating to see good food go to waste, she scrambled out of bed and, throwing a sweater on, made her way downstairs in her pajamas. Still bleary eyed from sleep, she didn't want to switch the lights on and stir herself fully awake. In any case, the square layout of the beach house made finding her way in the dark easy, although it helped to have the light of a full moon pouring in through the windows.

Eve fumbled with the front door handle, and then remembered she hadn't shaken off her city habit and needed to unlock it from the inside. As she turned to search the hallway table for the key, something caught her attention.

Something moving.

A shadow across the window.

She held her breath and stilled, an instinctive reaction, she thought and most likely an overreaction. "It's probably nothing but the breeze stirring a bush or a cat making its way home."

A very large cat?

No, she thought and decided it was most likely her imagination. It would take her a couple of days to adjust to the quiet and solitude. Although, it wouldn't kill her to take care. When she stepped outside, she drew her arms across her chest and took a couple of tentative steps, her eyes skating across the surrounding garden.

When she heard a tree branch scratch against a window, she swung around looking one way and then the other, her eyes narrowed as she searched for a pair of luminous eyes. Her aunt didn't own any pets, but the neighbors' pets loved to visit.

A seagull called out what sounded like a protest.

"Just great. All I need now is the hoot of an owl."

She shivered. Her back teeth locked together and she quickened her steps, all her attention on reaching her car and scrambling back inside the house. She couldn't explain the overpowering feeling of knowing there was something out there. Eve repeated the *something* in her head because she didn't want to think about there being a *somebody*.

She also didn't want to think she was being silly.

She'd watched enough suspense movies to know bad things happened to the least suspecting.

As she reached inside the car to retrieve the package, she thought she heard footsteps along the pebbled drive. And that, she told herself, was way too close for comfort. She sprung out of the car. Stretching her neck, she peered one way and then the other.

Nothing. No one.

She stood there, her breath slowing to a shallow inhale, her ears straining to pick up the slightest hint of disturbance.

Again, nothing. Or probably something.

She had no trouble imagining someone also holding their breaths and waiting to see what she did next.

"Now you're really being silly."

She scooped in a big breath and scanned the surrounding area again all the while thinking she should be scared. At least, until she had a reason not to be scared. However, good sense told her she hadn't lived on the island in a while. She only needed some time to settle in and get used to it all.

Back inside the house, she made a point of checking the doors and windows.

"Only as a precaution," she said out loud wanting to hear the sound of her voice over the silence that hovered around her.

With everything securely locked, she drew in an easy breath and smiled. By the next morning, all would be forgotten. This was nothing but first night jitters alone in a house she hadn't lived in for a while.

Everyone knew everyone on this island. If the population increased by even one, news spread like wildfire. At least she had a tale to tell when Mira returned.

Her shoulders eased down and she laughed under her breath. Mira would probably toss the tale around and then dismiss it as too clichéd to include in one of her stories.

She made her way toward the stairs and sprinted up the steps even as a sixth sense told her to stop and look around.

She didn't.

If she had, she would have seen a shadow appear at the window again.

Chapter Three

AS PREDICTED, the next morning Eve had forgotten all about the previous night's close encounter with shadows, unfamiliar noises and imaginary cats.

She decided the best thing to do would be to settle into some sort of routine. Relaxation being at the top of the list. After unpacking, she toured the house, taking note of any changes or additions.

Her aunt kept a tidy house free of clutter but she enjoyed collecting furniture and was forever having chairs reupholstered.

Bookcases lined every available wall space with every book shelved by author and genre. The thrillers and mysteries with all their sub-genres were lined up along the hallway entrance and spilled onto the front living room. Then came the contemporary romances, followed by historical romances, and her aunt's particular weakness, fantasy. Vampires, shape-shifters, demons... She couldn't get enough of them. Those were shelved in the family room next to the kitchen—Eve's favorite room.

There were a couple of comfortable high backed chairs upholstered in cheerful shades of blue and orange and a couch by the fireplace, a preferred reading area during the winter months.

An assortment of antique desks was spread around the house with pens and notebooks ready for flashes of inspiration. The kitchen was small and practical. Cooking had never been a strong point with Mira Lloyd so Eve had expected to find the refrigerator empty but, to her surprise, it appeared to be well stocked with basic staples. Bread. Milk. Eggs. The remains of an apple pie and some fruit.

She frowned.

Odd but not entirely unexpected.

Whenever Mira went on one of her trips, she arranged for someone to drop in and check her mail and keep the place dust free.

Being of a generous nature, she encouraged them to help themselves to drink and food. Eve tried to remember if Mira had mentioned hiring anyone in particular. Her travel timetable varied so much she could never rely on the one person to be available.

Despite her eagerness to sink into relaxing mode,

Eve decided to trek out into town again and get some more supplies. Enough to then justify staying away and out of sight for a few days. While she'd given up the restaurant business, she hadn't given up eating.

In the clear light of day, the house looked magnificent with a fresh coat of sky blue paint and the usual beach house paraphernalia, including an old-fashioned life preserver with thick rope curled around it, scattered on the veranda creating a picture perfect postcard of a home by the sea.

As she drove off, she made a conscious effort to appreciate the pretty scenery. Houses were spread right throughout the island. Some were modest, others large and a few, quite luxurious. All were well cared for and maintained either by their owners or by gardeners. Walking trails crisscrossed the entire island, making it a walkers' paradise.

A few minutes into her drive, she spotted Patrick McKenzie out on a sauntering walk. She slowed down and waved to him. He didn't seem to recognize her. He stood with his hand shielding his eyes. Belatedly, he waved to her. Eve suspected it had been a token wave. Patrick had once revealed he devoted his walking time exclusively to thinking and could collide with someone he was intimately familiar with and not recognize them.

In town, she hurried along to the grocery store only to remind herself to slow down. She'd already seen several people stop and look at her, as if wondering if they too should be hurrying... or running for their lives.

Relax and blend in.

She ran the words through her mind and focused on setting a leisurely pace, casual enough to let her do some window browsing. Drawn by a familiar sight, she stopped. Mira's fame was celebrated on the island and Tinkerbelle's Bookshop reserved the entire front row for her, displaying a selection of her Elizabeth Lloyd historical romance novels.

Eve bit the edge of her lip. Her aunt had always known she wanted to be a writer, penning her first story at sixteen. Eve couldn't help feeling a little envious. The thought of having to recreate herself at thirty-two, to find the energy and get up and go enthusiasm, made her stomach tighten with apprehension.

Soon, she'd be on a deadline.

She'd sold her restaurant for a small profit, enough to fund some thinking time, but not enough to give up working altogether. Like it or not, her clock was ticking.

She pushed out a breath. Some people went through several career changes throughout their lives without breaking into a sweat. She only needed to do some digging and find out if she had any viable skills she could use that didn't involve cooking...

About to turn away her eyes landed on a sign hanging on the front door of the bookstore.

For sale.
All inquiries welcomed.

She nearly tripped as a part of her took a step away and another part pulled her toward the bookshop.

Caving into temptation and the lure of the unknown, she went inside and spent some time browsing and getting a feel for the place.

For a small business, it carried a full range of stock covering all possible tastes, and going by the conversation she overheard, the shop owner was only too happy to place special orders. At least she assumed she was the owner.

Eve looked at her name tag. Abby.

She looked cheerful and relaxed. Serving a customer and having a lovely chat, she was all smiles. It would be a lovely change to work in an environment where she could smile instead of shout out orders as one was bound to do in a busy commercial kitchen, Eve thought.

"Can I help you with something?"

Eve turned toward the sales assistant who stood nearby. Business had to be good if the store could pay for staff.

"This looks like a lovely place to work in. Are you here full-time?" She knew it was an odd question to ask, but curiosity got the better of her.

The young girl, Samantha, smiled and nodded. "I'm

hoping the new owner will keep me on. There aren't that many opportunities in town and I had to wait a year for this job to become available and that only came about because the previous salesgirl got married and moved to the mainland." Samantha held her gaze for a moment. "Are you looking to buy a business on the island?"

Without trying too hard, Eve drew a mental picture of herself owning a bookstore and living on the island and decided she liked it.

"It's just become a pipe dream. I'd probably have to kill someone for the money." She didn't think the tidy profit she'd made from the sale of her restaurant would be enough to sink into another business. She imagined buying a bookstore would require a huge outlay as well as a final decision on what she wanted to do, right along with a dose of serious commitment. Would she be happy settling down here for the long haul? At least she'd be living close to Mira.

"Well, if you happen to find a pot of gold, get in touch with Abby," the salesgirl said and handed her a business card.

Before she could fill her head with dreams that would only depress her, Eve thanked her and left. However, for a brief moment, she'd bought into the idea of settling down here. The thought made her smile again so she didn't entirely dismiss it. Even fanciful dreams deserved to have their moment in the sun. No harm done. Especially if they made her smile and she hadn't had reason to do much of that lately.

She stood outside a moment gazing at the For Sale sign and tried to embellish her dream.

Maybe that was the push she needed. If she spent some time on it, she'd have a clear idea of something she wanted. And if she focused on it often enough, she'd somehow... someway... figure out how to get it.

"You're looking very pleased with yourself."

She looked up and saw Henry Parkmore scowling at her. He'd kept his voice low enough so that only she had heard him. Despite having retired many years before from his prestigious job in finance, he continued to wear suits, although he'd swapped his Brooks Brothers for English Tweet to satisfy his anglophile preferences, as Mira had often remarked.

His thick eyebrows slammed down so hard a wedge formed between his eyes.

Had he just remembered her theft of his roses? He'd made her pay for her crimes. For the duration of her stay with her aunt that long ago summer, Eve had had to drag around endless bags of manure for Henry Parkmore's roses and pull out every single weed before it had even sprouted.

"What have you done with my Mira?"

Eve's mouth gaped open.

His tone had never sounded so menacing.

She tried to fish around for a response but came up empty.

A woman strode past them and his demeanor changed in the blink of an eye, his manner softening as he dipped his head and greeted the local.

"Henry."

Just as Eve took a step back a younger version of Henry Parkmore without the fierce scowl came up to him and tugged his arm.

"Is everything all right?" the man asked.

"Yes, of course. Why wouldn't it be?" Henry Parkmore's gruff tone returned. He pulled his arm away and strode off in a huff.

The man turned to Eve. "I'm sorry... I hope he didn't say anything to upset you."

"No, no." What could she say? Henry Parkmore had been rambling and still looking for his pound of flesh because she'd stolen his roses? "Shouldn't you go after him?" she asked even as she watched the elderly man stop to talk to a passer-by.

Her eyes widened. He was doing it again. Pointing his finger her way, and this time it looked like an accusatory jab.

"He hasn't been himself lately," the man said. "Not many people know this. My uncle had a stroke earlier in the year." He shrugged.

"I'm sorry to hear that." Her gaze skated over the man. Dressed in jeans and a light sweater she'd swear was cashmere, he had the sort of preppy look some men never seemed to grow out of that reminded her of Alex. "I didn't know he had a nephew."

"I'm Richard Parkmore. I haven't seen you around. Are you new?"

"Sort of. My aunt lives on the island. I'm Eve Lloyd." When they shook hands, she tried not to notice the firmness of his grip, but that only left her wide open to focus on his dazzling blue eyes and easy smile.

Her divorce had drained her of any interest in men. However, Eve had never thought of herself as a diehard cynic. She imagined she'd eventually cultivate a more mature outlook and then be ready to move on. It never hurt to look, she thought, and went right ahead and enjoyed what she was seeing.

"I'm visiting too. Although I'm thinking of settling down in the area... to be close to Henry. Apart from my mother, he's the only other relative I have."

Eve's practical mind took over. "And what about work?"

"I'm on vacation."

From what, he didn't say.

"This is going to sound strange, but I get the feeling I know you from somewhere. I live in New York, on the Upper West side and—"

"I owned a restaurant on Columbus." She looked over his shoulder. "Henry's on the move again. Maybe you should go after him."

"Um... Yes. Great to meet you. I'll... see you around."

He actually waited for a response so she gave what she hoped was a noncommittal nod.

Eve turned to leave only to encounter Abby, the owner of Tinkerbelle's Bookshop standing a step behind her.

"Henry's getting worse. For a moment there, I thought he was pointing at me." Smiling, she introduced herself. "Hi, I'm Abby Larkin. I noticed you earlier in my store."

"I'm embarrassed to admit it was my first visit," Eve said, "My aunt owns a lot of books, which makes buying them unnecessary. Not exactly music to your ears." Eve smiled. "I'm Eve Lloyd."

"Any relation to Mira?"

"She's my aunt."

"And she's my biggest customer as well as draw-card. Interested in buying?" She gestured with her hand. "Don't mind me. Forget I said that. I'm desperate enough to approach anyone passing by with a hard sale."

"You might not want to spread that around. Looking desperate could bring down the price. I recently sold my business and pretended to only want to sell to the right buyer."

"You're right but I can't help thinking this place is too quiet. We need something to put us on the map." Abby tilted her head. "I don't suppose you have time for a coffee? I could do with some sound advice."

Chapter Four

EVE FELT she'd found a friend in Abby—her easy going manner something new to her. She couldn't remember the last time she'd sat down with a woman close to her age and had a carefree conversation. Pity Abby wanted to leave the island. She'd never been married and had decided to seek greener pastures before her time ran out and she ended up on the shelf.

"You lived in Manhattan, right there in the hub of all social activity," Abby had nearly screamed out. "And now you're here... in Rock-Maine Island because..."

"Great place to think," Eve had said.

"If that's what you're after, you'll get plenty of it here. And I don't need to tell you why that is, but just in case, I'll remind you. There's a population of just over a thousand and everyone is either married, about to be married or simply too old."

"Fine by me," Eve had said. "The less distraction, the better."

While she'd enjoyed the company, once again, her time alone had been delayed.

Despite her eagerness to get on with the task of relaxing, when she reached the beach house, she set her groceries down on the front veranda and went around the side of the house to see how close the bushes and trees were to the windows.

While Mira cared about the inside of her home, she never bothered much about the garden, letting it grow wild before calling in a gardener to prune back the bushes and tree branches.

She trudged along the side path. It all looked tidy enough. Kicking off the sand on her shoes, she looked down at the ground.

And that's when she saw the footprints.

Several of them and two different sizes.

Her own and another set...

Much larger. Twice her size.

And all directly under the living room window.

The path running along the side of the house led straight to the beach. While it wasn't a public thorough-fare, maybe someone had come up this way to cut through to the main road.

A couple of times she'd been caught out on a walking trek, which had turned out to be beyond her abilities and she'd had to double back cutting through one of the neighboring paths.

Frowning, she strode over to the end of the house and looked out to the shore. The alternative, for anyone walking along the beach, was to clamber over the breakwater that ran the length of Mira's property and continue on to the other side.

Then she remembered the previous night and the shadow she thought she'd seen. Had it been a local wondering if someone had broken into her aunt's house?

People in the area took their neighborhood watch seriously.

Then again, a local would have announced themselves and checked to make sure she had a right to be in the house.

She didn't want to think she was overreacting.

She let the idea settle and collecting her groceries carried them inside, but as she closed the front door, she heard the back door slam shut.

Eve dropped her bags instantly and acted before thinking, sprinting toward the back end of the house.

"Grab something," she told herself through gritted teeth and snatched a rolling pin.

She wrenched the back door open and raced out, no thought given to her safety as she rounded the corner and kept going until she reached the front veranda, her breath coming in short, choppy bursts.

Just then she heard the back door slam shut again.

Eve turned, her eyebrows drawing together.

Moments later, she was back inside.

She stood there watching as the back door creaked open again and slammed. Eve rolled her eyes. She'd left the security latch unlocked so instead of locking up automatically, the door remained open.

The slightest breeze would disturb it.

She lowered her shoulders and drew in a deep, calming breath.

Enough, she thought. No more thinking of shadows and strange noises.

"Hello. Mira?"

The sound of a voice calling out gave her a new understanding of the meaning of nearly jumping out of her skin.

With her heart thumping madly against her chest, she held on to the rolling pin, swung around and strode with purpose coming to a sudden halt by the fireplace. A young woman stood opposite her, her hands hitched on her hips.

"What the heck happened here?"

"That's what I'd like to know," Eve said.

An entire bookcase sat empty, all the books strewn across the sitting room floor.

Someone had been in the house.

"Who are you?" it finally occurred to ask.

"I could ask the same question."

Eve gave the young woman a raised eyebrow look and tried to take in her appearance just in case she needed to describe her to the police. In her mid-twenties, she had short-cropped hair the color of an expensive sable fur coat, large chocolate brown eyes, a pert nose and a smug smile that spoke of attitude.

"I'm Jill Saunders. I do occasional work for Mira." She returned the raised eyebrow.

"I'm Mira's niece. Eve Lloyd."

The girl's smile relaxed and turned sincere. "Oh. I should have recognized you from the photos. I've dusted them often enough." She turned to the mess on the floor. "Any idea how this happened?"

"I think I just surprised an intruder."

"A break-in? On the island?" Jill chuckled. "Not likely."

"And why not?"

Jill gave a small lift of her shoulder. "Everyone knows everyone."

"Well, I'm here and not everyone knows me. You didn't."

"Did you just put yourself under suspicion?" Jill asked.

Eve watched as she bent down to pick up the books. "I don't think you should disturb the evidence."

"You're kidding."

"Your fingerprints will be all over the books now," Eve reasoned although, if she thought about it, fingerprints probably didn't stick to book covers. Or did they? "Are you trying to cover your tracks?"

"Seriously? Surely, you're kidding. Mira never said you had a sense of humor."

"I don't, generally. This is serious. I just came home and walked in on an intruder who fled out the back door."

"And you chased after them with a rolling pin?"

Eve set the rolling pin down and started picking up books. "I'm not stupid enough to go out there empty-handed."

They stacked the books into neat piles, setting them aside to reorganize later.

"I'll put them back myself." In reality, Eve wanted to have a look through them. Whoever had broken in, had been after something and they'd thought to look through the fantasy section. Specifically, or had they intended working their way through all the books? Eve gave the girl a cursory glance.

"What?"

"Strange that as I chased someone who fled out the back you should then appear through the front."

"Back to that, are we?"

Eve blew out a huff and straightened. "I'm making some coffee. Would you like some?"

"Sure." Jill reached into her back pocket. "I brought the mail in."

Eve looked down at the envelopes. "Is that what you came for?"

"No. I just thought I'd use it as an alibi. In case someone asked."

Eve stared at her unblinking eyes. Finally, Jill laughed.

"You should see the look on your face. Honestly, if I wanted to steal something, I think I'd chose my moment better."

"I get the feeling they weren't here to steal something. Those picture frames are made of silver. They'd be worth a lot more than these paperback books." What would someone hide in a book? Her aunt treated them as tools of the trade, but she still looked after them taking care not to dog-ear the pages or crease the spines. Eve flicked through one. Mira would never dream of writing on the margins. Besides, what could she write that would be valuable to a thief?

The plot to her next bestseller?

Eve laughed under her breath and got busy making the coffee.

Her aunt did well out of her writing. Otherwise how could she afford to take so many trips? Those were her one and only real luxury. She owned a car, but it was over ten years old. She'd inherited the beach house from a spinster great aunt. Her basic needs were all met but, in all honesty, Eve didn't think she was swimming in money.

She handed Jill a mug of coffee and went in search of some cookies.

"Mira never mentioned you were coming to stay," Jill said.

Eve turned to face her. "Surprised by my presence, are you?" She stopped, a sudden flash of inspiration catching her attention. "Come to think of it, how come you didn't know Mira was away?"

"I've been visiting my granny in hospital. Only got back this morning. She broke her hip, poor dear. My folks are on a road trip, otherwise they would have spent time with her."

"So, you came back to the island and straight here, without stopping anywhere else?" Eve asked.

"If I'd stopped somewhere, I would have found out about you. Someone would have mentioned it." Jill chuckled. "Are you interrogating me?"

"Just answer the questions. Or are you trying to hide something?"

"Why would I? Mira employs me."

"Greed is a great motivator."

They stood there for a moment, measuring each other with belated wariness.

"Don't you think we should call the police?" Jill finally asked. "Or are you trying to hide your tracks?"

"Why haven't you called the police?"

"I'm still in shock."

"So am I." Eve drew in a deep breath. "I think we both need to back off now."

"You started it."

Eve nibbled the edge of her lip and wondered if this was a police matter. "I'll call them and report the incident in the morning. I've had enough. Honestly, I came here for some peace and quiet and look at me, I'm all wound up." When Jill didn't say anything, Eve threw her hands up in the air. "I don't see what difference it could possibly make if I call them now or wait until tomorrow. The police might not even come. They have more serious business to take care of. This might just be the work of kids with nothing better to do."

Jill finished her coffee and washed the mug. "It's your call. I have to get back to my own place. I've got two dogs to walk and they don't like to be kept waiting. Nice meeting you."

Half an hour later, Eve was relaxing in her bath when a thought occurred. If Jill hadn't known about Mira being away, why had she come by to collect the mail?

Chapter Five

THE NEXT MORNING, Eve finished stacking the books back on the shelves, taking care to put them in the right alphabetical order. The thought of her aunt returning home and finding the place turned upside down put her on edge. While she was staying in the house, she felt responsible for its upkeep. More importantly, she didn't want her aunt worrying. About anything.

Despite promising to call the police to report the break-in, she decided against it. As far as she could tell, nothing had been taken or broken, so she saw no reason to pursue the matter. She put it down to her toughened city exterior. In the city, this would be considered such a minor incident it wouldn't be worth anyone's trouble... Not that she had any experience with break-ins...

With the last book in place, she sunk down on the couch.

"Now to relax. And this time, I mean it."

She tried to ignore the events of the last couple of days, but her mind had other ideas. One after the other, bits and pieces whirled and chased each other around, filling her head with too many thoughts.

The footsteps in the middle of the night.

The door slamming shut.

...Your timing is unfortunate.

Who'd said that? At the time, she hadn't thought much about it, but now... it all took on a different meaning.

Had it been Henry Parkmore?

What have you done with my Mira?

Eve sprung upright. That had come from Henry Parkmore and what had he meant by 'my Mira'?

As far as she knew, there'd never been anything between her aunt and Henry. In fact, Mira thought he was too obdurate and disapproving.

Easing back down, she pulled a quilt over her and drew in a deep breath and another and another until she felt her body relaxing. She had to stop winding herself up. With that thought in mind, she eventually drifted off to sleep.

She had no idea how long she slept for. In the end, the incessant ringing of her cell phone woke her up. When she answered the call, there was no response.

"Probably a wrong number." She stretched and

yawned and feeling much better, decided to focus on thinking about nothing. "Nothing but food." She hadn't had lunch but she didn't feel like putting too much effort into anything so she settled for eggs and some toast.

Jumping to her feet she headed to the kitchen and, after a brief search around, she gathered the ingredients together.

She cracked a couple of eggs and popped a couple of pieces of bread in the toaster. Tidying up as she went, she felt her body relaxing. She'd given up cooking for a living, but it remained a part of her and would always bring her pleasure.

The thought faded. She looked up.

Pushing a sigh filled with resignation, she went back to the sitting room, her steps uncertain, hesitant.

She really should have called the police.

Even if they didn't do anything about it, they'd probably want to know, just to keep track... tally up the numbers. Use the information for some useful statistical purpose such as increasing police presence in the area.

She couldn't remember there being a law enforcement office on the island so the call would go through to the mainland, maybe to an understaffed precinct.

She stood there looking at the phone.

Snatching it off its cradle, she pressed it against her ear, only to put it down again.

The phone had an inbuilt answering machine and the

day she'd arrived, she'd left a message. A message she hadn't erased because she'd been too busy running around trying to get things done so she could finally sit quietly for some much needed thinking and therapeutic relaxation.

The message light should have been flashing.

But it wasn't...

She dug her cell phone out of her back pocket and dialed Mira's number. Immediately, the house phone rang. She waited for the machine to pick up. When it did, she said, "It's me. Testing. Testing," and hung up. Sure enough, the message light came on, flashing a bright, alarming red.

Drawing in a hard breath, Eve hit the play message button to make sure everything was working properly and then she pressed the delete button.

Someone had deleted her message.

The same someone who'd broken in and scattered all the books on the floor looking for who knew what?

As she took a step back, her cell phone rang.

"Yes," she answered without checking the caller ID. The way she felt right then, she'd happily talk to a telemarketer. There was no response. "Hello." Again. Nothing. Nothing but the silence of someone listening to her, she couldn't help thinking.

So much for emptying her mind.

The smell of burning eggs had her rushing back to

the kitchen. Snatching the frying pan, she dumped it in the sink. She'd never been so careless in the kitchen. She was a trained chef and could juggle a hundred and one tasks and still keep an eye on her kitchen crew.

Eve brushed her hands across her face. "This is ridiculous." As if to make it more so, the phone rang again. Except this time, it was the house phone. With a loud groan, she snatched it and barked out a greeting.

"Hello, who's this?" a smooth voice asked.

"Eve. Eve Lloyd. Who are you?"

"Helena Flanders. Mira's travel agent. I'd like to speak with her, please."

"My aunt is not home."

"Could you give her a message. I'm just calling to say there'll be no problems booking her into her Mediterranean cruise next month."

Alarm bells set off. "Hang on. Why are you calling now? You know she's not home."

"Why would I know that?" Helena Flanders asked.

"Because you're her travel agent and Mira is away on a trip. Presumably organized by you. That is, if you really are her travel agent."

"Of course I am. Who else would I be?"

"Where are you?" Eve demanded and heard the woman's hesitation. "Sorry, I didn't mean to snap, I'm... I'm just a bit confused about my aunt's whereabouts." Saying it out loud made it all too real. Mira always let her know before going away, but this time, she hadn't. Why hadn't that raised alarm bells with her?

"I'm at my office. In town. You can't miss it. We're next to the bakery."

"I'm coming right over." Eve hung up, snatched her jacket and car keys, and rushed out the door. Something was definitely not right. She'd drive into town, speak with the travel agent, by then she'd have more information and could feel more confident about paying a personal call to the local Sheriff's office. Possibly to report something more significant than a break-in.

Shortly after, she parked her car outside Tinker-belle's Bookshop and scanned the length of the main street for the travel agent's office. Glad to be wearing her comfortable loafers, she trotted down the street not caring what anyone thought. Right next to the bakery she could see a sign waving happily in the light breeze. An airplane.

Peering through the window, she saw several desks arranged in the rear with a few comfortable chairs out the front. A young woman rose to her feet, collected her handbag and stepped out of the building. Eve decided she was too young to be Helena Flanders who'd had the sort of raspy voice that came from years of smoking.

Eve strode in and was about to call out when a stylish woman appeared from the back. Dressed in a beige suit, a silk scarf in subtle shades of blue and green floating after her, she approached her, her lips stretched into an easy smile.

"Hello. You must be Eve."

Eve frowned at the easy recognition.

Helena laughed softly. "I'm not expecting anyone else today and I can't say that I've seen you around, so I'm going to assume you're the person I spoke with on the phone a short while ago."

"Yes," she managed.

Helena offered her a chair. "You sounded concerned."

"It's about my aunt. I'd assumed she'd gone on a trip organized by her travel agent, but you don't seem to know anything about it." Eve heard herself talk and cringed at how odd she sounded.

"If it's any help, I last spoke with Mira five days ago. She mentioned being on deadline and having to wrap things up but she didn't mention anything about going on a trip."

"But she's going on a cruise."

"Yes, next month. She wanted to finish a book and start working on a couple of outlines for a new series she'd been thinking about for a while. I can't wait. I love her novels. All those swoon worthy heroes..." Helena was about to sit down when she hesitated. "Would you like some coffee?"

Eve shook her head. "I'm already on edge. Any more caffeine and I'll be climbing walls."

"If she's not answering her phone, maybe she's out of range or in... what do they call it?" Helena snapped her fingers, "Her writing cave."

Her phone? It hadn't occurred to her to try her aunt's cell phone. Eve sunk back in her chair and laughed. "You'll never believe this."

"You haven't called her?"

"No. I'm so embarrassed. Fact is, I only became concerned about my aunt when you called earlier." She pulled out her cell phone and tried Mira's number. The call went straight to voice mail. She left a message for Mira to call her. "Well. That's that. Now to wait."

Helena checked her watch. "How about an early dinner? I'm finishing up for the day and can't be bothered cooking for myself. Would you like to join me?"

"I doubt I'll be good company."

"Nonsense. It'll take your mind off."

To her surprise, and despite everything that had gone on the last couple of days, Eve relented.

The island's small population didn't really justify having five restaurants. However, during summer the place packed up with people from the city trekking out for the weekend or the entire season. A couple of the restaurants actually closed up as early as fall, but three remained open all year round merely switching the menus to winter fare.

To Eve's surprise, Helena had come to live on the island after her own divorce. Before that, she'd run an exclusive travel agency catering to executives wanting to squeeze in leisure time with business trips.

She was well traveled and more than happy to be rid of her cheating husband, and ecstatic to do some mixing of business and pleasure herself, the island catering to her need to set a more leisurely pace, not that she ever considered retiring even though she was pushing fifty.

"You know there aren't many prospects on the island."

Eve had no trouble following her meaning. "I'm not likely to be on the market for quite some time, if ever. Mira never married and she's happy."

"She's the exception. Besides, she lives for her books."

"And her traveling."

Helena raised her glass. "She's one of my best clients."

Half way through their main course, they heard sirens blaring in the distance.

"Police?" Eve asked.

"Sounds like it. It's a record for them. That's the second time today I heard them. I've lived on the island for two years, and I've never heard them before today."

A wave of murmurs rose and fell in the restaurant. A few glances were exchanged and cell phones pulled out.

"Any idea what that was about?" Helena asked a passing waiter.

"It could be another intruder," he said. "Word is Richard Parkmore called them earlier today saying someone had broken into his place while he and his uncle were out on a walk." He shrugged and moved on.

Eve clasped her hands together and belatedly thought she should have reported her own break-in...

"I was thinking of skipping dessert but now I'm going to have to wait this out and see if news reaches us," Helena said, "It's likely to, you know. I'm still considered a newcomer, but even I know news always spreads like wildfire on the island."

Chapter Six

EVE REALIZED she had to rethink her entire strategy. So far, she'd been going about it all wrong. If she wanted to relax, she really had to stop trying.

Over the last couple of days, she'd made some headway only when she'd taken the time to socialize. First with Patrick McKenzie. Then with Abby Larkin. And tonight, with Helena Flanders.

News hadn't reached them after all. In fact, by the time they got to dessert they'd almost forgotten about hearing the police sirens.

An hour later, they parted ways promising to keep in touch.

She hadn't heard back from Mira. Eve supposed her aunt would return her call when she emerged from her thinking tank.

Instead of hurrying home, she drove slowly, her

gaze skating across the night sky. She couldn't remember ever seeing such a clear indigo blue sky filled with millions of twinkling stars, the vastness reducing all her concerns to nothing.

"It's the small pleasures in life that matter." If she focused on them, she'd make them her point of attraction and invite more pleasurable moments into her life, she thought and felt herself smile with ease.

After stopping a couple of times to gaze at the stars, she eventually made her way home.

As she pulled into the drive her smile dwindled and then froze.

Her heart gave a loud thump, picking up speed and using her chest as a punching bag.

A man strode toward her with purpose, his stride easy, in a swaggering sort of way, his arms raised, his hands palm up effortlessly directing her to stop.

He came around to the driver's side and waited for Eve to emerge from her car.

She took her time unbuckling her seat belt, her eyes flitting around as she tried to make sense of the scene in front of her aunt's house.

A police car had pulled up alongside the drive while an ambulance had been driven all the way up the front path. A police officer stood with his legs apart on the front veranda, his hands behind his back, another came around the side. And then there was the one waiting for her to emerge from her car. At least, she assumed he was a police officer. The others wore uniforms while this man sported a jeans and jacket casual look.

He took a step toward her and she imagined he was about to tap on the window when she pushed the driver's door open and slid out. Her legs gave a slight wobble so she held onto the door.

"What's going on?"

"I'm Detective Jack Bradford." He produced his badge. "Mind telling me who you are?"

"Eve. Eve Lloyd. I'm staying here." She pointed at the house as if her words had failed to convey the message. "This is my aunt's house. Mira Lloyd."

"Do you have any identification?"

"What's going on?" she asked even as she leaned inside the car to retrieve her handbag. She pulled out her license and handed it over.

The Detective drew out a small flashlight and pointed it at her license and then at her.

Eve flinched. "Would you mind not doing that?"

"This way please." He gestured toward the house.

Eve took an awkward step forward and then stopped. "What's going on?"

"That's what we're here to find out, Ms. Lloyd."

He gave another firm gesture pointing toward the house. He stood a head taller than her. Eve noted an easy manner about him, the sort that came with a great deal of confidence. He had a solid build, muscular without being overly bulky. Not that she even thought about it, but if she tried to run, she knew he'd only need to reach out and grab her.

Lifting her chin, she focused on moving her feet. All the lights had been switched on in the house. Beyond the windows she saw people moving about.

Stepping up to the veranda, the officer standing there slid his gaze toward her. Eve felt tremors of uneasiness running along her legs and settle in her stomach.

Not Mira.

No. Nothing had happened to Mira.

It couldn't have.

She was away somewhere thinking and plotting her story outlines and possibly feeling guilty about not returning her phone call...

Her step must have faltered. She felt a steadying hand curl around her elbow. The detective guided her inside and toward the front living room.

"Would you mind taking a seat?"

"Not until you tell me what's going on," she said finding her voice while at the same time sinking into a chair.

Another officer approached and drew the detective aside.

Without thinking, Eve erupted to her feet and rushed out of the living room.

"Hey. Stop," someone called out.

She reached the kitchen and that's when she stopped.

Right there, on the light gray slate floor of her aunt's pristine kitchen she saw a body, arms sprawled out, legs apart in a caricature of a chalk outline.

Her body stiffened.

Eve gasped and clamped her hand over her mouth.

Her gaze jumped from the man to the bright blue frying pan she'd used earlier to cook her eggs. The eggs that now sat sunny side up on the man's head.

Eve took a stumbling step back and collided with a stone wall. Or rather, a very firm chest.

"Is there something wrong with your hearing? I thought I asked you to stay put."

She swung around, her eyes charging up to fire Detective Jack Bradford with a blast of her resentment when she noticed the person sitting by the fireplace.

Eve peered around him and saw Jill, her legs curled up beneath her, her hands wringing together. When she lifted her large doe like eyes, her lips trembled. Her face was chalk white.

"Jill."

"I guess you two know each other," the detective said.

"What are you doing here, Jill?"

The young girl managed to lift her hand and point toward the kitchen. "I—" She crumbled and buried her face in her hands.

Eve turned to the detective, this time her eyes managed to blast him with a fierce glare.

"What's going on? Who is that?" As the words spilled out, she turned and forced herself to look at the body again.

The shoes.

Brown suede with a flashy gold crest on them.

She'd recognize them anywhere.

After all, they'd been purchased with her hard earned money.

"Alex," she said, her tone hard.

"You know the victim?"

"Victim?" Resentment surged through her. Eve swung around to face the detective. Even when dead, Alex could garner sympathy. "Alex isn't... wasn't a victim. He was always the perpetrator."

The detective held her gaze.

"He was my husband." Her chin shot up in defiance of what she'd been forced to admit. "My ex-husband."

The detective's attention shifted away from her. He gestured with a nod. Eve turned around in time to see an officer removing the eggs from Alex's head and slip them into a plastic bag.

Evidence, she couldn't help thinking, followed by the reminder that Alex had never liked eggs, any which way, and that had made cooking for him extremely difficult.

She responded to the tug on her arm, her feet moving automatically. Moments later, she found herself sitting in the front living room again, the detective taking a chair opposite her. Within minutes, she watched as the ambulance officers wheeled Alex away.

"Would you like something to drink?"

Eve found the offer odd coming from a stranger. Shouldn't she be offering to make pots of coffee?

She shook her head. "What happened?"

"We received a call from Jill Saunders. She found the body."

Jill?

"Would you mind telling us where you were today?"

Us? She looked up as if to confirm there was only one of him. She supposed he meant us, the law enforcers.

So, what did that make her?

The suspect?

Eve slid to the edge of the chair. "I did not kill Alex."

"Okay."

"I was having dinner in town. With Helena Flanders."

"Is she a friend?"

"She's the local travel agent. I wanted to ask her about my aunt's whereabouts. Mira Lloyd. This is her house."

"Your aunt is missing?"

"No, I mean... I don't know." The sound of a vehicle reversing had her twisting around to look out the window. The ambulance was leaving and taking her ex-husband's body away.

Alex. Dead.

In Mira's house.

"So, which is it?"

"What?"

"Your aunt. Is she missing or not missing?"

"She's away. Except that I didn't know she'd be away. She usually... always tells me when she goes on a trip."

"And this time she didn't."

"She's an author," she said as if that explained everything.

"Jill Saunders says she does general house cleaning for your aunt."

"Yes." Or at least, that's what Jill had also said to her.

"She also said she came around to help you clean up after your house was broken into."

"And that's when she found Alex?" Eve had only

been out for a couple of hours. "When did all this happen?"

He held her gaze long enough for Eve to think he didn't really care to be at the receiving end of questions.

"We haven't established that yet. Perhaps you can help us out. What time did you leave the house?"

"I don't know. I rushed out." She explained about the phone call she'd received from Helena Flanders. "I guess it must have been before five. Helena's office was still open and businesses usually close at five. I noticed one of her staff leaving just as I was arriving at the travel agency." Eve brushed her hands along her thighs; something the detective seemed to take note off. She clasped her hands together. Didn't nervous people fidget with their hands?

Nervous... guilty people.

"And then you went to dinner."

"We heard the police sirens. We were about to be served our main course... no wait... we were half way through our main course. An hour later, we parted ways."

"Did you drive straight here?"

"Yes."

"It took you half an hour to drive in from town? It's only a five minute drive."

"I drove slowly."

"I there a reason for that?"

"I'm trying to relax."

He frowned.

"I'm here to relax," she threw her hands up in the air, "And look what's happened."

"You sound inconvenienced."

"Well, wouldn't you be if you were trying to relax?"

He stretched a leg out, gave his trouser a tug and sat up again. "About the break-in—"

"What about it?"

"Why didn't you report it?"

"This is going to sound strange, but I didn't take it seriously. I'm from the city and—" She raised both shoulders. "It didn't really seem that important."

"Someone breaking in, not important? Jill Saunders said you'd chased after an intruder."

Jill Saunders had been saying a lot of things.

"I heard Richard Parkmore reported a break-in at his place." She waited for him to say something. For a long moment, he held her gaze as if trying to re-establish some boundaries.

"Where did you hear that?" he eventually asked.

"At the restaurant. Word spreads quickly on the island."

"Did word reach you about your husband's death? Is that why you took your time returning to the house?"

"What? He's not... he wasn't my husband. Alex and I divorced a year ago." Her gaze dropped to his chest.

She counted the times it rose and fell before he spoke again.

Five easy breaths.

"When you recognized him, you sounded angry."

"I thought I was rid of him once and for all. And here he was again—" Dead on her aunt's kitchen floor. "He hated eggs."

Again, she counted his breaths.

Five.

"You're a chef."

"Did Jill Saunders tell you that too?"

He looked at her arms. Specifically, at her forearms. They were strong. Not in a bulky way, but she'd spent years handling heavy pots and pans...

Eve supposed he'd again breathed five times.

"Cast iron frying pans are quite heavy," he said.

Eve brushed a hand over her forearm and tugged at the sleeve that only reached her elbow.

"Do I need to call a lawyer?"

Chapter Seven

EVE WAS under strict instructions to stay on the island and available for further questioning.

She hadn't bothered to explain that she had nowhere else to go. Her apartment had been sublet for six months. While she'd planned on visiting her aunt for at least a month, she'd had no idea what she would do with the rest of the time she'd allotted for the launch of the new Eve Lloyd.

After everyone left, Eve stood in the middle of the living room wondering what to do with herself. The detective had asked if she wanted to stay somewhere else, or if there was someone she wanted to stay with, but she'd insisted she would be fine.

Crime scene tape prevented her from going into the kitchen. Something she found absurd since the police appeared to have done a thorough job of collecting samples of everything, including the contents of the trashcan.

Making the rounds of the house, she looked out the front window and noticed a squad car parked outside.

Did that mean they didn't trust her?

Was she under suspicion?

Had she put herself under suspicion by asking if she should get a lawyer?

She sat for a long while in the dark trying to gauge how she felt about spending the night alone in a house where a man had been killed.

The fact she'd mentally referred to Alex as a man suggested she was already trying to distance herself from the incident as a way of coping with the experience.

For a long time, she'd hated Alex but never enough to want to see him dead.

Not really.

People had their faults.

Alex more than his fair share.

As far as Eve was concerned, if she couldn't accept a person's faults, then the only solution was to find distance. Wasn't that what her parents had done with her?

Eventually, she fell asleep curled up on the bed. Sometime during the night, she must have woken up enough to pull a quilt over her.

Alex. Killed. "Murdered."

Those had been the first thoughts she'd had when she woke up the next morning and they stayed with her for the remainder of the day, spinning around in her mind.

Stepping out of the shower, she raked her fingers through her hair.

Who would want to murder him?

She dug around the closet looking for something appropriate to wear as if the occasion called for something special.

She was a widow. By default.

Should she wear black?

With an impatient shake of her head, she selected a pair of faded blue jeans, black boots and a cream cable sweater. And since she couldn't access the kitchen, she grabbed a jacket and set out to find herself some breakfast.

Annoyingly, she wondered if her appetite would work against her. Surely it would indicate a clear conscience. Although.... shouldn't she be more upset?

As she got in the car, she continued to wonder how her actions would be perceived.

"Oh, stop it." As if people would expect her to go hungry just because her ex-husband had been murdered.

Who would kill Alex?

Everyone liked him. In fact, despite his embezzlement, she'd actually... sort of... still liked him.

He'd been a charming man. Polite. Friendly. Engaging. A great conversationalist.

Murder just didn't make sense.

It happened to other people. It was the sort of incident you read about or watched on a long running crime TV series.

She'd bet anything money was behind it all.

That had been Alex's long-standing fault. Caring more about money and the lifestyle it could provide him.

Driving past the squad car, she slowed. The officer barely glanced her way. As she drove off, she noticed he remained at the house.

It didn't mean she was off the hook. When she reached the town, she encountered another squad car. It tailed her until she parked her car.

She went into the Chin Wag Café, making a point of sitting by the window within sight of the parked squad car, a part of her wishing to be accommodating and cooperative.

A tap on the café window had her looking up.

Abby Larkin stood there holding a handful of books under her arm.

Eve waved and signaled for her to join her.

"Hi." She was all smiles but her eyebrows drew down into a slight frown. "I've never seen so many police cars. Everyone's talking about it. They're saying it has something to do with Richard Parkmore reporting an intruder yesterday."

"You haven't heard."

"What?"

Eve caught her up giving her a brief rundown on everything that had happened since the day before.

"Your ex? Dead? In your aunt's house?" Abby leaned forward and lowered her voice. "Did you kill him?"

"As if I'd tell you if I had." She took an impatient sip of her coffee. "It's such an inconvenience. I can't even use the kitchen."

"Eve. How can you say that?"

"Well, if you'd known Alex, you'd understand. I can't figure out what he was doing on the island. I haven't seen him in two years. Suddenly, he's there. Dead. And I'm being interrogated." An image of Detective Jack Bradford popped into her head and she felt her body flush.

"What just happened? Did you think of something? Your face went all red."

She sighed. "Have you seen the detective in charge?"

Abby shook her head. "I've never even been issued a parking fine. I'm a law abiding citizen."

"What does that make me?"

Abby gave an easy shrug. "A suspect, of course."

"Please don't joke."

"I wasn't. I've read enough crime thrillers to know you have to be realistic. The finger's pointing straight at you. You knew the victim. He was killed in your home."

"Right. So, I lure my ex-husband to the island, kill him, and then trot off to have dinner."

"Perfect alibi and perfect blasé attitude." Abby sat back. "It's what I'd do. Play the innocent card. Go on as if nothing had happened."

"He was killed with a frying pan. My fingerprints will be all over it."

"You should be more thorough with your washing."

"I'll keep that in mind next time I plan to kill some-one." She drank more of her coffee and eyed Abby over rim of the cup. "You must be pleased."

"Why?"

"This is bound to put the island on the map. As far as I know, there's never been even a ripple of scandal. Suddenly, you're desperate to sell your bookshop and you complain about the island needing to be put on the map. This will definitely do it for you."

"What are you suggesting?"

"Careful what you wish for because you might get it, by fair means or foul."

Abby stretched her arms out. "Do I look like the type of person who'd commit murder?"

"Don't assume there is a type." Huffing out a breath, Eve pulled out her cell phone and the card Detective Jack Bradford had given her and called him.

His gravely tone had her holding her breath. "Hi, it's me. Eve. I'm calling to see if you've found the murderer yet. I'd like to have my kitchen back, please."

She lost herself in the sound of his voice. "You don't sound at all sorry for the inconvenience. In fact, I get the feeling you disapprove of my request." She shook her head. "Yes, of course I'm available all day for further questioning. You'll know where to find me. I'm sure your officers are lodging regular reports of my where-abouts, as if I had anything to do with Alex's death."

An hour later, Eve sat in the living room looking straight into Detective Jack Bradford's sharp blue eyes.

"He deserves to be murdered," he read from his notepad.

"Who said that?"

"Apparently, you did."

"When?"

"Over dinner at the pub, two days ago you told Patrick McKenzie—"

She held her hand up. "Isn't this where you step down and hand the case over to the CSI?"

The edge of his lip lifted.

"Of course not, I'm sure you already realize how ridiculous it would be for me to have killed Alex."

"You had reason to dislike him."

"I had reason to hate him. And I even had reason to want him dead. I dare you to find a woman going through a tough divorce who wouldn't entertain the same thought."

His eyebrows quirked up.

"I didn't mean to say that to Patrick McKenzie. It was a slip of the tongue. I was decompressing."

"You've been stressed?"

"You don't know the half of it. Alex nearly destroyed everything I'd worked so hard to achieve, I had to work day and night to pay off our creditors with only half the staff, the other half I had to let go because I couldn't afford to keep them on, and don't get me started on how that made me feel."

"How did that make you feel?"

"Like killing him, of course," her voice hitched, "It's only normal."

His eyebrows rose again.

Eve drew in a long breath. "If I had killed him, I wouldn't be saying that. Surely you can see that?"

"I only work with facts, Ms. Lloyd."

She gave an impatient shake of her head. "Shouldn't there be someone else here with you to take turns?"

"Take turns?"

"Good cop, bad cop. Come to think of it, shouldn't we be doing this at the precinct?"

He sighed and flipped his notepad shut. "We appreciate your cooperation."

"But?"

This time, he frowned. "It appears your ex-husband had some serious money problems."

"Well, I could've told you that. It was never enough for him."

"According to his phone records, he'd been in touch with you."

She shook her head. "I haven't spoken with him since well before the divorce."

"And yet you received a call from him yesterday. Two, in fact."

It was her turn to frown.

"Is there something you want to share with me?" he asked.

"There were a couple of calls, but no one spoke." She held his gaze and remembered to blink. "I guess you'll have to take my word for it."

"How are your finances now?"

"Isn't that a bit personal?"

He tapped his notepad against his hand.

"I'm comfortable."

"I assume your aunt has named you the sole beneficiary in her will?"

"I've never asked and—" she shot to the edge of the chair. "Why bring my aunt into this?"

"You expressed concern for her whereabouts. You've tried to contact her. Has she returned your call?"

No, she hadn't.

Eve shot to her feet. "I'd like to report a missing person."

Chapter Eight

BY LATE AFTERNOON the next day, the crime scene tape had been removed from the kitchen and Eve distracted herself with scrubbing the kitchen from top to bottom. When the phone rang she thought the call might be from Mira and rushed to pick it up without bothering to remove her bright yellow scouring gloves. "Yes?"

"It's Jill."

"I have a bone to pick with you," Eve snapped.

"What did I do?"

"Hang on, I have to think." So much had happened, she'd pushed everything to the furthest corner of her mind. And then it came to her. "Why did you tell Jack about me not reporting the break-in?"

"You're on first name terms with the detective?"

"Saying Detective Jack Bradford is a bit of a mouthful, don't you think? Anyway, answer my question."

"He asked and he's got this way about him. I think it's his eyes. They're gorgeous. And his voice, there's something compelling about it. It's the sort of voice you want to hear murmuring in your ear in the middle of the night."

"He's too old for you."

"And he's just right for you?"

He could be. The thought was enough for Eve to believe she was on her way to eventually trusting a man again, or at least giving him the benefit of the doubt. She'd decide when and if an opportunity opened up. "Be serious. A man has lost his life."

Jill chuckled. "I was about to remind you of that."

"What do you want, Jill? I'm busy cleaning up."

"I rang to find out how you were, and this is the thanks I get."

"I'm sorry I snapped. Come around. I could do with the company."

"Do you think that's wise? Us being seen together."

Eve had trouble deciding if Jill was being serious or trying to make light of the situation. "I'm not really under suspicion. Are you?"

"I'm on my bike. Meet me at the bottom of the path, the one that trails off the side of the house."

"You didn't answer my question."

"Why would I be a suspect in a murder investigation? I didn't even know you before yesterday and I had no knowledge of your husband's existence."

Jill had known of her but hadn't met her in person. "I'm sure there's a loophole in there somewhere," Eve said under her breath. "All right. I'll meet you in ten minutes."

She tore off her scouring gloves and grabbed a jacket. When she made her way along the path at the side of the house, she realized she remained out of sight of the squad car still parked out on the road. Had Jill chosen this path deliberately?

Eve's step faltered.

Reason told her Jill had nothing to do with Alex's death. But murder rarely stood the test of reason.

It all came down to motive.

She didn't know anything about Jill other than what she'd told her. She cared about her granny and her dogs. She had to be reliable otherwise Mira wouldn't have hired her. But even innocent people could lapse...

She trudged her way along the narrow path carved out by daily walkers and noticed how alert she'd become. Her eyes scanned the area as she went and she felt a slight tightening of her shoulders.

At the bottom of the path, she narrowed her eyes and tried to make out a shape between the trees then she caught sight of movement and what might have been the reflection of a bicycle mirror.

Eve emerged onto a clearing and found Jill standing there, leaning against her bike. She wore black jeans, a black sweater and a black baseball cap tilted to one side.

"Traveling incognito?"

Jill pressed her finger to her lips, calling for silence.

"Is this where you tell me to follow you and you lead me to a trap?"

"You have a wild imagination," Jill whispered.

She led her to another clearing, which happened to be at the edge of a cliff. "Right, this is definitely as far as I go. I hope you don't expect me to stand close to the edge."

Jill stood there gazing out to sea and then turned to her. "Richard Parkmore is having money problems."

"How do you know that?"

"I heard him say so." She set her bike down and came to stand next to Eve. "I was out walking my dogs last night and I heard a voice. I crept up—"

"You do that often, do you?"

Jill ignored the remark and looked around them. She lowered her voice. "I saw Richard Parkmore standing right here talking on the phone."

"And that's not allowed?"

"When he finished, he hurled the phone over the cliff."

Now, that was odd. "Maybe it had outlived its use."

"Exactly." She stabbed the toe of her sneaker on the

ground. "Before that, he went on and on about how tight with money his uncle was."

"And that makes him a suspect. Are you suggesting he killed Alex out of frustration because his uncle won't give him a weekly allowance?"

"I think there's something significant about the conversation I heard. It can't have been coincidence. Somehow, it has to be linked to... something."

"Sounds to me as if you're forcing the dots to join. You think he killed Alex because of course he knew him from way back—" Eve frowned. Hadn't Richard Parkmore mentioned recognizing her?

They'd lived and worked in the same area in the city. Maybe he'd come into the restaurant. He might even have been a regular. Maybe he'd known Alex. In fact, when she'd first met Richard, she'd compared him to her ex. Richard was just the type of man Alex hung out with, all full of themselves and pretending to be more than they were...

"Did I happen to mention I'm here to relax?" Eve rubbed her neck. The knot there had tightened. "Everyone has money troubles. Living in New York doesn't come cheap." And Richard had mentioned coming to live on the island so he no longer had that concern. In fact, living here probably cost him nothing.

Eve folded her arms across her chest. "How are you holding up?" After all, Jill had found the body.

"I haven't been sleeping much," Jill said, "I've no idea how you could stay in that house knowing someone's died there."

"The house is over two hundred years old. Many people have died there."

"You're very pragmatic."

"And you see something wrong with that?" She brushed her hair back. "It's a coping mechanism. Honestly, if you really think about it, someone, at some point in time must have died right on this spot where we stand."

Jill jumped back. "*Eww.*"

"Did you tell Jack about Richard Parkmore's phone conversation?"

"Nope."

"Why not?" Eve noticed Jill's breath was coming hard and fast. Was she scared?

"I've had other things on my mind."

"Such as?"

Jill bit the tip of her thumb and again looked around them. Almost as if trying to make sure no one was around to hear them. "You left a message on Mira's answering machine."

Eve slammed her hands on her hips. "It was you. You erased the message."

Jill nodded. "Only after I listened to it."

"When?"

"The same day I met you. I'd actually popped in earlier. You were out, but I noticed there was something odd about the house. You know that feeling of someone having just left a place. Maybe it was your perfume lingering in the air. Anyway, I listened to the message and erased it by mistake. It just happened automatically. I do it all the time at home because if I don't the machine fills up. Anyway, I panicked and left. Then I felt guilty and decided to go back to see if you'd returned. I wanted to explain, but then there was the break-in, so it slipped my mind."

Eve searched her mind trying to remember the message she'd left for Mira. She'd been so tired from her long drive, and thinking about spending time in this out of the way place and having to make so many decisions...

She'd left a message saying she was coming to stay. And then she'd said something else. What had it been?

Eve groaned.

Mira had spent her entire life writing about love. She had made the Beatles' song her motto.

All you need is love.

And that was the last thing Eve wanted to hear about.

She loved her aunt, and her well-meaning ways but sometimes, her positive outlook could be too much. It had been a year since her divorce had become final, but the wounds remained fresh. She simply wasn't ready.

I'll kill you, Mira.

"You know I didn't mean it," Eve finally said.

"That's what you'd say, of course."

"Are you thinking of blackmailing me?"

"More pancakes?" Eve offered.

Jill shook her head.

"Still refusing to talk to me?"

"Throw in some dinner and I'll rethink my silent treatment."

"Which you just broke."

"How else am I supposed to bargain?" Jill set her fork down. "I still can't believe you think me capable of blackmailing you."

"It makes sense. You're young. You don't appear to have a real job. I know Mira is generous but you can't be earning enough to make a decent living."

"I live with my parents. It doesn't cost me anything. And—" She lifted a forkful of pancakes to her mouth.

"And what?"

"These pancakes would have been so much better with blueberries."

"If I'd known I was going to have to make peace

with you, I would have stocked up on blueberries." Eve poured herself another cup of coffee. "You were going to say something else before."

"I paint."

"As in art?"

She nodded.

"Did you go to art school?"

"I'm self-taught." Jill drained her cup and gestured for more. "Go on, ask me what you really want to know."

"Are you any good?"

"My paintings sell."

"That's wonderful. You should be living in New York right in the heart of the art scene."

"I don't paint the sort of pictures you see hanging in museums. I do pretty beach scenes. The tourists love them. And I'm happy painting them."

"How did you get into it? Is it like a hobby?"

"Sort of. I actually went to college. Graduated top of my class. Got an internship at a fashion magazine. Then I burned-out."

"What?" she asked even as she tried to digest everything Jill has just revealed.

"It all got too much for me. The highly competitive environment. The backstabbing. The constant monitoring of one's appearance. The constant bickering over who was getting ahead and who wasn't. I exploded. It got to the point I didn't even want to get out of bed. I came back to the island and one day I picked up my mother's paint brushes and started dabbling with painting."

"How exactly did it get too much for you at the magazine?"

"Everything fell apart for me. I came undone and developed an eating disorder. It wasn't so bad because I didn't go into denial about it."

"Oh."

"Anyway, painting makes me feel good and I earn enough to keep my parents off my back. Although, it all goes a bit quiet in the winter." She shrugged. "So, you see, I have no real need to blackmail you." Jill finished her pancakes and washed the plate.

"Are you doing okay now?"

"Huh?"

"Stupid question, I just saw you stuff yourself with a stack of pancakes."

"Oh, yeah. I'm okay." Jill drained the last of her coffee. "You really should be careful what you go around saying. You can't leave messages like that or go around telling people you wanted your ex dead."

"Are you trying to teach me how to avoid being a suspect?"

"More like how to avoid being thrown in prison for a crime you didn't commit."

"It's so comforting to know you have my back." Eve looked down at her hands. "When I left that message for Mira, I'd been frustrated. It's a long story."

"What about what you said to Jack? Your whole attitude was wrong. The police are on the lookout for slip-ups and you seem to be happy to deliver them."

"I was upset. I'd just seen the man I thought I was going to spend the rest of my life with lying on the floor dead."

"It must have been horrible."

"Horrible doesn't begin to describe it. I'm still waiting for the aftershocks. They're bound to come." She pushed out a breath. "Anyway, it can't have been a picnic for you either."

Jill nodded. "I nearly tripped over him.... and I screamed. I never knew I was a screamer. My throat still feels sore."

They sat in silence for a while.

"Why would you say you wanted to kill Mira?"

Eve sighed. "If we're going to have a tell all session we'll need more coffee." Eve got up but instead of making coffee, she went in search of pen and paper. "It won't take long to tell you about Mira's matchmaking ways and how frustrating I find them. After that, I think we need to start drawing up a list of suspects. Someone killed the man I once loved, and I need to get to the bottom of it."

Chapter Nine

"THERE'S SOMEONE AT THE DOOR."

Eve sprung upright, her arms flailing, her toe connecting with the coffee table. "Ouch. Who said that? Ouch. What the—"

"Me." Jill peered down at her from the couch. "How was sleeping on the floor?"

"I can't feel my back. What possessed me to give up the comfort of my bed... or the couch?"

"It was too late for me to go home last night. I refused to sleep downstairs alone and you lost the coin toss and had to crash on the floor. Personally, I think you should have been a better host and just offered me the couch without resorting to a coin toss. And that's someone pounding on the door."

"I'm coming," Eve called out as she crawled on all fours. "Mira needs to get plumper cushions and guest sleeping bags." When she reached the front door, she stood up and said, "Whoever you are, unless you have coffee and donuts, you don't have any business being here." She drew the door open a fraction and peered out.

"Good morning."

"Detective."

"May I come in?"

"Do you have news about my aunt?"

He shook his head.

"How about news about who killed my ex-husband?"

Another shake of his head.

"No news, no coffee, no donuts. And now I'm supposed to let you in and offer you coffee?"

"It would be a generous gesture."

"So, are you here on official police business?"

"Always."

"Are you here to arrest me?"

He held his hands up. "I'd need a warrant for that."

She brushed her hair back only then realizing she still wore her yoga pants and an old t-shirt. Not exactly dressed to impress. Then again, she had no business thinking about wanting to impress a man who might end up handcuffing her. "Okay. Come in." She drew the door open and waved him in.

"Rough night?" he asked.

"The worst." They strode along the hallway. When

they passed the family sitting room, Eve noticed Jill wasn't there. Had she fled? Was she that serious about not being seen together?

"I make strong coffee," she warned, "If you prefer something less potent say so now, or forever hold your peace."

"Strong coffee will hit the spot."

"I'd offer you some French toast but I seem to be missing a frying pan. Any idea when I'll get it back?"

"At this stage, you might want to consider getting a new one."

"I was going to anyway." While she didn't feel that uneasy about being in the house where Alex had been killed, in reality, she had reservations about using the murder weapon to cook her eggs.

"Toast?"

He shook his head. "Just coffee, please."

She organized the coffee and looked over her shoulder. Something inside her stirred awake. An awareness of his male presence. He filled a room nicely. And he smelled great. She drew in a breath and inhaled a hint of fresh soap and a musky aftershave lotion.

He stood by the door leading to the sitting room.

"Looks like you had a busy night."

"Do you take sugar and cream with your coffee?" she asked as a way of drawing him back to the kitchen. Last night, she and Jill had sat down to a brainstorming session filling countless pages with notes and questions marks.

"I take mine black, thanks."

She looked out the window in time to see Jill scampering away. Clearly, she didn't heed her own advice about suspicious behavior.

"Here you go." She handed Jack a mug.

He turned to her, his face expressionless as he held up a piece of paper. "What's this?"

"I see you're in detecting mode."

"Eve."

He'd called her Eve. What had happened to Ms. Lloyd? She didn't care because suddenly, she liked the sound of her name on his lips. She pressed her mouth against the mug and mumbled, "It's a piece of paper."

"With a name on it. My name."

"Well... just because you're the investigating officer doesn't let you off the hook."

"What?"

"How convenient for you to be called out here to the scene of a crime soon after you left the scene yourself. The moment you step in, you contaminate the scene with your DNA which will be disregarded because you're the officer in charge."

He held her gaze without blinking. "You have an overactive imagination."

"Or perhaps I'm more savvy than the average bear.

Which goes to show I'm innocent. Otherwise, I'd be playing my naïve card."

"What exactly do you think you're doing?"

"Trying to clear my name. I might or might not end up spending more time on the island and I want to be able to walk with my head held high," it occurred to say. "There's a mantle of suspicion hanging over me, and don't try to deny it." She waited for him to deny it, but he didn't.

"You haven't answered my question," he said.

"I did. It's not my fault if you're not satisfied with my answer." She blew out a breath. "I'm doing my civic duty by providing a different perspective." Eve smiled as she suddenly imagined breaking the case.

"Eve. Careful, you're playing with fire. A man has been murdered and the killer is still out there."

She'd never actually thought about it in those terms. There was a killer on the loose and he could be watching her. Right that minute.

He? How about a she?

"So who else was here with you last night?" he asked.

"No one."

"Are you sure about that?"

"Are you asking me to revise my answer?"

"You've been watching too many TV shows." He

looked around the room. "And reading suspense thrillers."

"The books belong to my aunt and she's not here so you can't point the finger of blame at her."

He drank his coffee in one gulp.

"Did you bother to even savor that coffee?"

He nodded. "Very good. Gourmet?"

"Yes. I picked it up at the Chin Wag Café. They have a surprisingly good selection."

He sighed. "I'd advise you against getting involved, Eve."

"But I am. There's no escaping the fact. I'm right in the thick of it."

"You know what I mean. Don't go sticking your nose where it doesn't belong."

"What do you think I'll do?"

"Go sniffing around where you shouldn't," he insisted, "At this stage, we don't have a clear lead."

"So anyone and everyone on the island is under suspicion."

"The only new person reported—"

"Is me and the victim, my ex-husband. Which begs the question, why am I still free?"

"Are you putting yourself forward as a candidate?"

"I'm just surprised at how quickly you dismissed me as a suspect."

"You sound offended."

"I'm only concerned. Just how thorough are you being? What if something now happens to me? You know what they say about disasters coming in threes. Alex has been killed. My aunt is possibly, we don't really know, but maybe missing..." She didn't wait for him to answer... or not answer. "Am I being framed? Did someone try to point the finger at me in a not too subtle way? Are they now waiting to ambush me?"

"You used to own a restaurant."

She had the feeling he'd just diverted her attention. "Yes."

"How do your employees feel about you?"

"We had a great professional working relationship."

"What about the ones you let go?"

So, he'd heard about those and that meant she had been considered a suspect. She lifted her chin. How dare he... "I gave them glowing references and used my contacts to get them new jobs." Belatedly, Eve realized she'd already mentioned having to let people go...

"What about the people on the island? Is there anyone who might resent you being here?"

"I can't think why. My aunt is loved and appreciated by everyone. And I haven't ever lived here long enough to cultivate friends or enemies. The only—" She set her mug down, her coffee splashing on the kitchen counter.

Henry Parkmore would have to be deranged to enact

some sort of vindictive backlash for her theft of his roses all those years ago.

"You were about to say?"

"Nothing."

"Eve."

Your timing is unfortunate.

She suddenly remembered Patrick McKenzie had said that. His choice of words seemed extraordinary... just because she'd chosen to appear out of the blue, unannounced.

What had he meant?

"No one knew I'd be coming here." She walked around the kitchen, her gaze on the floor as if that could provide her with some clarity.

Her aunt was missing. Not really, but hypothetically, she could be. What if something had happened and Patrick had done away with Mira. There could have been an argument brought on by a long overdue declaration of his feelings for her. Eve imagined Mira laughing it off. Something no man would appreciate. It could have triggered something in Patrick. A scorned lover's rage. There could have been a struggle.

She strode to the window and gazed out at the breakwater.

What if they'd been standing outside? Patrick could have been overcome by a sudden surge of uncontrollable passion, grabbing Mira, hauling her against him.

Shocked by his uncharacteristic behavior, Mira would have tried to break free. In her struggle, she might have slipped and fallen into the water. She could have hit her head and...

Died instantly.

Her body floating away and sinking fast...

Shock. Disbelief would have quaked through Patrick and he would have had a few seconds to decide what to do.

Seeing her dead body, knowing it had been an accident but feeling confused and contrite he would have decided no one would believe him. His first reaction would have been to flee.

As he made his escape... on foot, he would have fallen in step with his usual habit of thinking. And that's when he would have contrived a plan to clear himself of any wrongdoing.

Patrick would have assumed he'd have time to work out the details.

Time for the body to be eventually discovered.

But then Eve had arrived unexpectedly, thwarting his plans.

Eve nodded as if agreeing with herself.

Yes. Her sudden appearance could have foiled Patrick's plan to let some time pass before reporting Mira missing.

Your timing is unfortunate.

What if Patrick had then set out to pin a murder rap on her? It wouldn't be difficult to cast all suspicion her way. If she could kill once, she could kill twice. And if she had no compunction about killing her aunt, she wouldn't think twice about doing away with her ex-husband.

Without thinking too hard about it, Eve knew Mira would name her as the sole beneficiary in her will. All these books, Eve thought, would be left to her... Mira had no other relatives and no inclination whatsoever to leave her worldly possessions to her sister, Eve's mother, who would probably turn the books over to the nearest thrift store. There might also be some money...

Eve pressed her hand against her throat.

And that would take care of the motive.

There were some people on the island who knew she would welcome more money. The subject had come up at the bookstore. Eve had told Abby's assistant that she'd have to kill someone to be able to afford to buy the bookshop.

"Eve?"

She held her hand up calling for a moment longer.

She turned her thoughts back to Patrick McKenzie and tried to dig beneath the layers of his outward friendliness.

Would he be capable of murder?

Could he orchestrate a plan to cover his tracks?

He was a serious thinker and had a fount of knowledge he could tap into.

Patrick had met Alex a couple of times during Eve's visits to Mira. He could have used their acquaintance, finding a way to contact him to lure him to the island.

Patrick might have been the shadow she'd seen the first night she'd arrived...

He might have been keeping an eye on her comings and goings. As soon as Alex had turned up, he might have led him into the house as an excuse to corner him in the kitchen where Patrick could use the one weapon Eve would resort to.

A kitchen knife...

Or a frying pan.

"I think you were right. Alex was a victim."

Chapter Ten

"WHY DID YOU RUN OFF AGAIN?" Eve asked Jill. As soon as Jack had left right after he'd once again warned her to keep her nose clean and right out of trouble, Eve had pulled herself together and left the house to go in search of Jill. They'd bumped into each other at the bakery where Jill had just purchased a bag of donuts.

"I was hungry and didn't think you'd feed me breakfast."

"You expect me to believe that? You're scared and you're hiding something."

Jill picked up her purchases and swirled away.

Forgetting why she'd gone into the bakery, Eve chased after her. "Wait up."

"I'm in the middle of a painting frenzy and just popped in for a quick fix of donuts. Sorry, I can't hang around."

"Then I'll follow you."

"You're doing it again, Eve. Everyone can see you're chasing after me. If something happens, you'll be suspect number one."

"Because?"

"We're having a public altercation."

"Grab your bike and throw it in the back of my car. I'll drive you over to your place."

"That'll defeat the purpose of me trying to avoid being seen with you."

"That's what I thought," Eve grumbled, "So I'm forcing your hand."

"Or else?"

"Or else, I'll tell Jack you've been scurrying around and acting suspiciously." Although, Eve suspected he already knew that, hence his questions about who else had been in the house with her.

"What do you want, Eve?" Jill asked as she secured her bike in the back of the car.

Eve waited for Jill to hop in the passenger seat.

"If you must know, I got spooked." Mostly by her own thoughts and mental images of Patrick McKenzie declaring himself to Mira and then accidentally killing her. "Jack has been trying to find someone who might hold a grudge against me. The thought unnerves me. I'm a good person and someone's made me a target."

"You might be good, but you're also pushy," Jill said.

"And you think some people would find that reason enough to want to hurt me?"

Jill shrugged. "Ours is not to reason why."

"I'm not pushy. I'm just... stressed." She checked her mirrors and drove off at a sedate pace.

"You keep saying that. Stress can impact your behavior. Again, you should be careful what you go around saying."

Eve tapped her fingers on the steering wheel. "All right. I don't want to be alone. I'm starting to see everyone in a new light."

"Including me?"

She hadn't thought of that. "Needs must. I can't be suspicious of everyone. Besides, I figure if I spend a day away from the house, I'll stop thinking about what happened."

"So, you want me to distract you. What if you hadn't bumped into me?"

"I was on my way over to your place... and I came to the bakery to get you some donuts."

Jill shifted in her seat. "I suppose you could pose for me."

"Didn't you say you painted beach scenes?"

"You could be a figure in the distance, pondering your next evil act."

"Just so long as no one recognizes me. Although, if I'm framed for killing Alex, you could make a killing with the tourists. I'm sure there's a market for that sort of art. Come to think of it, that could be a strong motivation for wanting to frame me."

Jill groaned. "Are you getting ideas about me again?"

"I have been thinking about people who might benefit if they had me out of the way. For starters..."

Jill gave her a lifted eyebrow look. "Yes?"

"Hang on, I have to think about it." If she went to prison, Mira would disinherit her.

Then Patrick could step in and marry her because of course, Mira would be heartbroken and susceptible to Patrick's romantic attention...

Now, there was an idea worth considering.

The thought tugged her in a different direction.

What have you done with my Mira?

Eve gasped.

"What?"

"I can't dismiss Henry Parkmore. He's always had it in for me." And she suspected he too had a thing for Mira.

"I'd be more concerned about his nephew."

"What are you doing?" Jill asked as she strode into her parent's living room carrying a couple of mugs of coffee.

"Jack warned me not to interfere. He saw all the notes we made last night, so I have to stash them somewhere else. We can use your place as our headquarters." She spread several sheets of paper on the floor and stepped back to study them.

"I'm thinking I should have offered you chamomile tea instead of coffee. I swear this coffee is quivering with anxiety at the thought of being anywhere near you."

"Perhaps you're right." Eve took a sip of her drink and curled her lip. "This is awful. Did you use instant coffee?"

"I ran out of the good stuff."

"Remind me to get some more. If we're going to put in the time, we'll need sustenance."

Jill sunk down on a couch. "So, who's your main suspect?"

"So far? Everyone."

"That narrows it down."

"Spare me the clichés, please." Eve pushed her sleeves back. "We have to think like professionals and throw logic out the window. It serves no purpose in a murder investigation."

Jill dangled her foot over the armrest. "And you read that in the quick guide to solving a mystery?"

"It stands to reason. I'm going to start by discounting career criminals, if there is such a thing. I'm also going to assume this was a knee-jerk reaction killing and not premeditated. It happened because... because of my sudden appearance on the island. So, the killer is a regular person." She gave a firm nod. "People who suddenly turn to killing someone are likely to act out of fear or impulse. Therefore, they'd have no imme- diate justifiable reason. Nothing we would see as logi- cal. The act could possibly be an accident but, I insist, not premeditated." She tapped her chin. "My money's on... Let me think..."

"Abby Larkin," Jill offered. "She has the most to gain by a windfall. With you out of the picture, she could endear herself to Mira, get in her good books, pardon the pun, and stand to inherit the lot."

"Now you're thinking like me." Eve couldn't imagine anyone being so devious. Although... "That might not be as wild as it sounds. Abby said the island needed to draw attention. What better way than to have a murder take place here?"

"Right. Because someone looking to buy a business will be drawn by the notorious reputation of an other- wise dull little island," Jill said.

"It's not so far-fetched. She killed Alex just because

the murder would get a mention in the papers and not necessarily because she wanted to frame me. I think she actually likes me."

"You sound needy."

Eve rolled her eyes. "Where are those donuts you bought?"

Jill waved the bakery bag. "Do you have any friends outside the island who might want you out of the picture?"

Eve gave an impatient shrug. "Nope."

"Is that a no to friends or a no to friends with ulterior motives?"

All the friends she'd made at school had gone on to successful professional careers and Eve had fallen by the wayside as she'd pursued her interest in cooking, working up the ladder in one restaurant and then another. It had all seemed less than appealing to her high achieving friends who hadn't had the patience to wait for her to make a success of it. Of course, she'd met other chefs in training, but everyone had worked such odd hours, some even holding down a couple of jobs to make ends meet because entry level pay never seemed to be enough...

"I led a very busy life working day and night. It left little time to socialize. Don't judge me."

"I'm not. You seem to be friendly enough. At least on the surface."

And pushy...

She wasn't pushy. She liked to get results and, despite what her parents might think of her, once she focused on a target, she threw herself into succeeding.

Eve flung her hands out. "I'm all out of ideas here. Maybe we should talk about you again."

Jill laughed. "Right, as if I'd relinquish any pertinent information about myself that would put me away for life."

"It was worth a try. I need to recharge myself. How well is your kitchen stocked? My stomach's grumbling."

"You can use whatever you like. Just stay away from fried eggs."

"That wasn't the least bit amusing."

Eve had a scavenge through the cupboards and refrigerator and decided to make a Spanish Omelet, taking her time to chop onions finely and cut the potatoes into tiny cubes.

When she found a deep enough pan, she poured some olive oil in, waited for it to reach the appropriate temperature which she tested by tossing one cube of potato in. The oil instantly sizzled, so she lowered the heat and tossed in the rest of the potato cubes. Once they were lightly browned, she added the onions. As they cooked to a nice transparency, she cracked a couple of eggs, seasoned them with salt, pepper and some grated Parmesan cheese and whisked them to a fluffy consistency. Into the pan they went. She gave the mixture a thorough stir. Lifting the edge, she decided one side was cooked. Placing a plate over the pan, she tipped it over, sliding the omelet onto the plate and quickly back onto the pan to cook the other side. It only took another minute to finish cooking.

"You didn't have any lettuce mix. We'll probably get hungry in an hour."

Jill searched a drawer and pulled out a selection of menus. "Ever heard of take-out?"

"You can take the chef out of the kitchen, but at the end of the day, I'll always be a chef at heart. I'd rather throw something together myself." She cut the omelet into wedges and served them on small plates. "Now, where were we?"

"Either killing time because you don't want to be home alone or trying to fabricate evidence to pin on someone else."

"That's harsh. I'd never do that." Eve brushed her hair back. "Apart from enjoying your company, talking about this keeps me busy. Every time I stop thinking, I remember seeing Alex's body on the kitchen floor. He was only a couple of years older than me and now he's gone. Snuffed out in the prime of his life. It could just as easily have been me. Apart from Mira and possibly my parents, there'd be no one to mourn me. And if it had been me, I doubt Alex would have spared me a second thought. He was that self-obsessed. Although, he was charming, and every time I say that about him, I can't help thinking of the good times we had." She pushed out a quivery breath and slumped back in her chair.

"Are you all right?" Jill asked.

"Yes, I'll be fine. This is all so very morbid and my first encounter with death."

"Me too, but you don't hear me going on about it. And I found the body."

"I'm sorry about that."

"Why? It wasn't your fault."

"Nice of you to say so. Still, I feel partly responsible. There's no escaping the connection." Eve rose to her feet. "I'm going to make some muffins."

"Blueberry, please."

Half an hour later she was back in the living room going through all their notes, the aroma of muffins wafting from the kitchen. "What have we got so far?"

"So far, you've only mentioned people you've encountered recently. Do you think there might be someone you met during your previous stays on the island who might have developed an intense dislike to you?"

"I only ever got to know our immediate neighbors. Every time I came here, I stayed at the house. Mira loves to eat out, but when I visit, I always cook. Even when I was young. She actually loves not having her writing time interrupted by trips out."

"So we'll have to stick to everyone you've encountered recently."

She had to admit she'd been having fun these last few days chatting with different people, including Jack Bradford. The thought of anyone she'd recently met being in any way involved made her shudder with concern. How was she ever going to trust anyone again?

"Good heavens, I can't believe someone I've come to like could be a murderer."

Chapter Eleven

AFTER ANOTHER LATE night brainstorming session, Jill had offered Eve the guest room. Eve had to admit she'd slept better at Jill's house than she had in days. It helped to know there was someone else around.

She returned to Mira's house to shower and change and was about to step out again when Jack knocked at her front door.

"Going out?" he asked.

"Yes, are you going to hold me up?" She tried to ignore how good he looked in his sports jacket, his light brown hair windswept and the hint of a couldn't be bothered shaving stubble on his chin.

"I have a few questions for you."

"Come through. And seeing as you came empty-handed again, I'll make us some coffee." She strode off toward the kitchen and could have sworn her temperature hiked up a notch. Jack put a couple of steps distance between them, but she couldn't help noticing him even when she had her back turned to him.

When she swirled around, she noticed him looking at her in a way that suggested he had run his gaze from the top of her head all the way down to her shoes.

"New look?" he asked.

"My jeans are in the wash." Eve brushed her hands along her skirt. That morning she'd decided she could only brave the day if she wore her no-nonsense vintage Chanel suit, complete with a string of fake pearls and sleek sling backs. She only brought the ensemble out on special... serious occasions such as visits to her bank manager or accountant.

Also, she'd just washed her hair and it hung in glossy waves around her shoulders. She'd even gone to the trouble of dabbing on some make-up, something she rarely did because her mornings had always started so early with trips to the market to source stock for her restaurant...

Today, she meant business and she fully intended rolling up her sleeves and making some sort of head-way. There was thinking outside the box and then, there was looking at a problem with fresh eyes, something she believed she could do.

Yes, this was business.

Jack Bradford had trained eyes, but she had the

advantage of having lived with a man who'd given a new meaning to lying. Eve was sure she'd learned something about sifting her way through layers of deceit, even if it had come to her by osmosis.

"Was there something you wanted to talk to me about?" she asked.

"I've been tracking your husband's final days."

"Ex."

"Your ex-husband's final days."

"Let me guess. He spent his mornings at his health club where he swam his usual twenty laps, after which he had a massage, followed by a late breakfast at his favorite hotel, the Carlyle. How am I doing so far?"

"Spot on. No need to lure your ex here when you could have picked any one of his favorite haunts."

"He was predictable." Up to a point. She'd actually never seen the side of him that made him capable of stealing from her. All those years spent squirreling away money from right under her nose and she'd been none the wiser. But it wouldn't happen again. She couldn't make the same mistake twice because the second time it wouldn't be a mistake. It would definitely be a choice.

Jill had said she'd pointed the finger of blame at just about everyone she'd met. Maybe that had to do with the fact her trust had been severed. Was she going to go through life suspecting everyone?

She leaned against the kitchen counter and looked up at Jack.

His gaze held steady.

He wouldn't have anything to hide. Yet... he kept his thoughts well under wraps.

"What else did he get up to?" she asked.

"He had an appointment with his lawyer."

"I didn't know he had one. I certainly didn't until I was forced to engage one."

"Alex was there to draw up a new will."

"That suggests he had something to—" She pushed off the counter. "He siphoned off money from my restaurant to the point of sucking it dry and he was going to leave it all to someone else? Who? I'll kill her—"

Jack Bradford sighed. "He also took out a life insurance policy."

Eve sunk back against the counter. "He what?" That implied he actually had someone he cared about and as far as she knew, Alex... or at least the Alex she had come to know, only cared about himself. Of course, the divorce might have changed him. Just because it hadn't worked out between them didn't mean he hadn't gone on to entice someone new into his life.

"He named you as his sole beneficiary. In both the will and the life insurance policy."

"Me?" The word quaked through her. Eve felt her

face drain of all color. She counted her breaths until she got to five in the hope that she'd somehow emulate Jack's calm demeanor. "Out of curiosity, have you stopped interrogating everyone else on the island?"

"He had a nerve. How dare he think he could worm his way back into my good books by including me in his will and his life insurance policy." Eve fumed all the way to Jill's place. Once she got there, it was all she could talk about with Jill.

"So does this mean you are now officially suspect number one again?" Jill asked.

"Jack wouldn't say. I think he's setting me up and waiting for me to make a wrong move."

"He's devious," Jill said under her breath, "And I'm guessing he won't have long to wait."

"What was that?" Eve asked.

"Nothing."

"You deserve a medal for putting up with me," Eve said when she stopped long enough to draw breath.

"It's not as if you're giving me much choice." Jill gave her a small smile as she wiped a paintbrush clean.

"You never told me your paintings were abstract."

"They're not. They're atmospheric."

"I'll have to buy one from you. This one," Eve said

pointing at a rectangular frame. "It'll look great in my bedroom." It was a picture of a sandy yellow cliff with an endless horizon in deep azure blue. "It looks haunting. You have a delicate touch and I don't see why you couldn't display your work in a major art gallery. I'll have to see if I know someone who knows someone. That's how it works."

"It's not what you know but who you know?"

"Exactly."

"What's with the overnight bag?" Jill asked.

"Do you really need to ask? I also brought some food. I'm cooking lemon chicken and roast potatoes. Nothing fancy. I don't think you've been feeding yourself properly."

"Are you suddenly afraid of staying at your place alone?"

Eve shivered. "More so than ever before. I can't believe that double-crossing ex-husband of mine has now made me a real suspect. Even after death, he's still out to ruin my life." Eve strode around the room Jill used as a studio, stopping to study one painting and then another. "A suspect. Me."

"Did Jack say that?"

"No, but it was implied. I'm sure it was. Why else would he tell me about Alex drawing up a will and taking out a life insurance policy? He wanted to see my reaction."

Jill drew in a deep breath. "I'm almost afraid to ask what that was."

Eve shrugged. "I... I sort of jumped to conclusions."

"Yes..."

"I imagined Alex had a new woman in his life."

"And?"

"I said... I said I'd kill her."

"Oh, Eve."

"Well, wouldn't you say the same? The man lived off me all those years, stashing money away who knows where. When I find out what he's been doing, all hell breaks loose. We divorce because obviously I can never trust him again. It's only natural that he'd find someone else. Either to enjoy the fruits of his underhanded ways or... to find another target, another source of income. Anyway, the thought of him splurging on someone else did my head in. Scoundrel."

"Did he ever work?"

"He did, but his ideas were never the brightest. He imported wine and not always the best. He had one failed venture right after the other. That was his forte."

"I suppose it was only natural for Jack to look into your husband's activities but do you think someone might have nudged him in that direction?"

Eve stopped pacing and turned toward Jill. "What are you thinking?"

"I'm putting myself in the place of the real

murderer. I'd want to draw attention away from myself and like you, point the finger at someone else."

Eve thought about it and decided it made sense. "The killer probably wants a scapegoat and the sooner the better. The longer the investigation drags on, the higher the chances he'll get caught." She stubbed the tip of her shoe against the floor. "You think people on the island see me as guilty?"

"Don't take this the wrong way but the thought occurred to me. It's only fair."

"This isn't a tit for tat game, Jill. I never really thought you were capable of committing a crime."

Jill swung away.

"Then again..." Eve edged toward her. "You're taking this business of not being seen with me very seriously. Are you hiding something?"

"Why would you ask that?"

"You are hiding something."

Jill's shoulders rose and fell. "There was an incident. When I worked for the magazine. My boss was the devil in disguise. She made my life a living hell. I eventually cracked."

"And?"

Jill shrugged. "I discovered I had a temper."

"What did you do?"

"I'd worked so hard to climb up the ladder, doing all the rubbish jobs no one else wanted to do. Being the go-to person. Always reliable. Always ahead of my dead-lines. The job I was gunning for came up and she gave it to someone else because she didn't want to lose the person who always picked up after her."

"Yes? And?"

"She had a thing for white. Everything in her office was white. I snuck in one night and painted everything red."

"You saw red."

"And she pressed charges."

"Did this come up when Jack questioned you?"

"That's just it. He hasn't questioned me." She shrugged. "He had a few questions on the night of the murder but he hasn't followed up."

"And you're afraid he'll look into your past and pin the murder on you because you already have a record." Eve shook her head. "I wouldn't worry about it. You don't have the build. Whoever killed Alex had to be able to wield a cast iron frying pan. And look at you, compared to me, you're pint-sized." Eve folded her arms. "Stop looking at me. I did not kill my ex-husband. And spare me the cliché sitting on the tip of your tongue."

"The one about the lady protesting too much? You have to let me say it at least once. It's a cliché because people use it all the time."

"All right. But only once."

"To change subjects at the rate of knots, have you heard back from Mira?"

"No. I know I should worry, but I can't. Mira has her ways. When she says she wants to think, she means it. The fact she went away to do it only means she has serious thinking to do as well as some shopping. She'll probably come back with a hoard of purchases she won't even remember getting. I'm guessing it all has to do with this new series of books she's thinking of writing. Helena mentioned it."

"Helena, the travel agent?"

"Yes."

"How come we don't have her on the list of suspects?"

"Because she's... she's—" Eve couldn't think of a reason.

"What do we know about her?"

Eve shrugged. "She's content with her life. In fact, she's the only one I've met who doesn't seem to have a care in the world."

"That should make her a prime suspect."

Missing several ingredients for the dinner she'd promised Jill, Eve drove into town leaving Jill behind to finish up her work for the day.

In town, she bumped into Patrick McKenzie.

"I've been meaning to drop in on you but that nice police officer told me to stay put," Patrick said. "I've only come out now because I've run out of food. How are you holding up?"

"Very well, thank you, Patrick. And I don't think the police actually meant for you to stay locked up at home," she said, her tone concerned for his well-being. Instantly, she felt contrite for thinking Patrick could harm Mira and then go on to kill someone else.

"It didn't bother me. Who wants to be out and about when there's a murderer on the loose?"

"Is that how you feel?"

"It's how everyone on the island feels."

Eve hadn't stopped to think about that. It made sense. As far as she knew, this was a crime free island. Or, at least, it had been until she'd come along.

"Please tell me they're not talking about me."

"I can't say that I've heard anything. Then again, as I said this is my first outing in days." He waved her into the grocery store and followed behind her. "It must have been a shock to you." He reached out and took her hand.

"Anything unexpected is a shock. I was out having dinner. When I returned home the place was swarming with police." She looked at him in time to catch him flinching. "Then they started firing questions at me as if

I'd had something to do with it all. I suppose they questioned you too."

He nodded.

"Were you able to provide any information?" Other than echoing the remarks she'd made to him about Alex being a candidate for murder, she couldn't help thinking.

"Their line of questioning was very effective. I had to justify my every move for that day. I told them I'd spent most of it reviewing the line of succession of British monarchs. It's a little mental excise I do every now and then to keep my gray matter honed to perfection," he said and gave his head a tap. "By five o'clock that afternoon I was up to the reign of King Henry the Eighth, that's when I'd reached the edge of the path leading to your house and stopped for a break."

"Where exactly?"

"Near the cliff."

The cliff, where she'd had a rendezvous with Jill and where Jill had seen Richard fling his phone into the sea.

"And it was five o'clock."

"Probably later than that," he said, "I stood there for a while pondering the last days of Henry's reign, then I spent some time thinking about the brief reign of his son, Edward. In fact, I thought about him longer than I usually do before I moved on to Mary. She wasn't very pleasant so I'm never in a hurry to get to her. I'd say it was closer to five thirty."

"Did you see anything unusual?"

"The police asked me that."

"And what did you tell them?"

"That I'd been wondering what Henry the Eighth would have thought of his daughter's reign outshining his. Elizabeth, not Mary. And..." he looked up at a top shelf.

"And?"

"I took a step forward. You know, the way one does when one is thinking and I nearly lost my footing."

Eve clasped her hand to her mouth.

"My heart pummeled all the way up to my throat. I stumbled back and my gaze dropped to the beach below. I couldn't help thinking what a close call I'd had and that's when—" He turned to her, his finger raised. "Now I remember."

"What?"

"I saw a man." His brows beetled down. "Do you know, I'd forgotten that."

"Who did you see?"

He tilted his head as if in thought. "I remember wondering who it could be and thinking I'd have to get closer to the edge, but I was still shaken from my close call so I gave up and strode off. I always encounter someone on my walks, so I didn't think much of it."

A local? Walking on the beach...

Eve wondered if this was something Jack would need to know about. Patrick was right. People on the island were serious walkers. Jack would have to interrogate everyone. If he hadn't done so already...

Chapter Twelve

"EVE, WHERE ARE WE GOING?" Jill asked.

"For a walk." She'd spent the night and most of the next day thinking about Patrick's sighting of someone on the beach. She tried to remember what time he'd mentioned being there...

Five thirty?

The tide would have been coming in by then.

She'd often walked along the beach, but only on Mira's stretch. Patrick had seen someone out here that night. Had it been someone making his way to the beach house? Perhaps not for the first time?

"A walk. Yes, but where?"

"I want to know where this stretch of beach leads to."

Jill stopped. "Mira's house, of course."

"I know that. But can we actually get all the way to the beach house?"

"Only if you're game. We'd have to clamber over the rocks."

"So, from Mira's end we have the breakwater..." Eve tapped her chin. "And over the other side..."

"Another clearing and then the rocks. See, there they are," Jill pointed to a rocky outcrop that appeared to erupt from the sea. "The rocks are rough and hard edged and you don't want to be anywhere near them at the end of the day. It's hard to say how high the tide rises."

"You know, I never asked Jack if they'd determined a time of death." But she could somehow figure it out. "Helena phoned before five that afternoon. I can't say exactly when and by the way, she's not a suspect because she was with me all the time. Anyway... let's see, I'm going to work backwards." She scooped in a big breath. "I arrived at her agency at five o'clock. I remember seeing one of her staff leaving for the day. Soon after, Helena said she was closing up. It only takes ten minutes to drive into town. After Helena's phone call, I only took a couple of minutes to grab my jacket and car keys, so I must have left the beach house at four forty five. Or thereabouts. Let's say four forty." She frowned. "No, I'm sticking with four forty five."

"Why not four thirty?"

"No, it only takes ten minutes and I drove with purpose. Remember, I was concerned about Mira. All that time I'd assumed she'd gone on a trip and there was her travel agent telling me she knew nothing about it. So, I left the house at four forty... five and returned at..." As she tried to remember, a graphic picture of Alex's body sprung in her mind, so she switched it all off for a moment.

They continued on in silence. Seagulls hovered around them. The sea was calm and there was barely a whisper of a breeze stirring the air.

"There," Jill pointed up. "Up there is the clearing where I met you and presumably where Patrick had his close call."

Eve checked her watch. "I wonder how long it takes to reach the house from here."

"Do you think the man Patrick saw down on the beach was the murderer?"

Eve nodded. "It has to be. If the murderer had come in from the mainland, I would have encountered him as I made my way to town." Eve stopped and looked back. "This beach can be accessed from all the properties lined along the way."

"Including my parents'. Does that put me back on the suspect list?"

"Thanks for reminding me. What time did you get to Mira's house?"

"I guess that's a yes?"

"Time, Jill. Time."

"Well, I don't have a watch. Let me see, I'd taken the dogs out for their walk at five thirty. That usually takes half an hour. Back home at six. After I had something to eat, I felt restless. I couldn't find anything to watch on TV and I'd just finished a book and couldn't decide which one to read next so I thought I'd go over to your place for a get to know you better chat."

"You wanted to spend time with me?" Eve smiled. Jill was about ten years younger than her, but she was easy going and Eve had so far enjoyed her company.

"I get the feeling you have issues," Jill said.

"A full load of them on my shoulders," Eve agreed.

"Anyway, I hung around the house for a bit trying to decide if I felt like trekking out to your place. By the time I made up my mind, I could see the sun already setting. I probably spent another five minutes trying to convince myself it wouldn't be worth my while when I finally set off."

"It's a good fifteen to twenty minute walk from your place to Mira's, so you would have arrived at about—"

"I couldn't find the flash light to take with me along the path so I walked along the main road. I'm thinking maybe seven thirty. That's my guess."

"Okay. Now for Alex. At some point, he drove into the island and so that had to have been after five. Let's see, you arrived at seven thirty. So that gives the killer a two and a half hour window of opportunity to do his business. Let's say two hours because I'm sure that if he'd seen you coming, you wouldn't be here talking to me."

"Way to go, Eve. You're definitely staying with me tonight."

They continued walking, their feet leaving deep prints along the way. Eve couldn't help thinking about Alex being here on the island. If she'd seen him driving by, she might have been able to change the outcome. He might never have gone all the way to the beach house.

But he had.

Eve frowned. What if Alex had merely walked in on the killer rummaging through Mira's house? That theory would sever all conspiracy connections between Alex and his assailant. It would also clear Alex...

She wanted that for him. Whatever he'd done to her, she didn't want to spend the rest of her life thinking he'd been capable of doing something far worse like getting mixed up with the wrong type.

"Keep your eyes peeled," she said.

"For?" Jill asked.

"Anything. Something. Hey, maybe that phone you saw Richard Parkmore throw over the edge."

"A phone would sink, not wash up on the shore."

"We can't be certain of that." When they reached the outcrop of rocks, Eve stopped and followed a trail of seaweed that looked as if it had been collecting over time. "The water line only reaches half way up the beach so even with the tide up, you could still climb over the rocks. The killer could have made his way undetected."

"Don't forget Patrick. He saw him."

Yes, and he'd said it had been about five thirty. "But he couldn't be sure and he couldn't identify him. I doubt hc'd be able to pick him out of a line-up."

"What now?" Jill asked stopping at the edge of the rocks.

"We climb over."

"I'm wearing my best jeans," Jill complained.

"They're paint splattered."

"And your point is?" Jill asked.

"If anything happens to them, I'll buy you a new pair."

"And you'll put them through the wash a hundred times and smudge paint on them in-between washes?"

"If that's what it takes, yes."

"Did you know the Queen of England has her new towels put through the wash about fifty times to soften them before she gets to use them?" Jill asked.

"Don't tell me you're a trivia buff."

"My mother is and the fact I know this means she can never complain about me not listening to her."

"Watch your footing," Eve warned, "We'll go slow."

"Why? You don't care that you're putting my life in danger."

"I'm more concerned about you walking behind me. I should have frisked you for weapons."

"And I'm thinking we should have brought Misfit and Mr. Magoo along with us."

"Your dogs?"

"They're good at sniffing things."

"There wouldn't be any lingering scents for them to follow. It's been days." They made slow progress. Eve couldn't imagine anyone braving this in the fading light. One false misstep, and... well, she nearly twisted her foot. A bad twist would put anyone out of action.

With the tide coming in and the light fading, one would have to be extra cautious. And, Eve decided, quite desperate to get across.

"Eve, wait for me."

"You're supposed to be young and agile. What's wrong with today's youth?" She looked up and let off a whoop. "There it is."

"What?"

"Mira's house." Ahead of them, the beach stretched all the way to the breakwater and that would be easy to clamber over. The murderer could have come this way to avoid being seen from the road or any one of the paths crisscrossing the area.

"Question," Jill said.

"Yes?"

"Assuming the murderer came this way, he would have had to know you'd be out for the night."

"He could have kept vigil from here. Seen me leave the house." Although, they'd already decided he had to have come this way after five thirty, the time Patrick had spotted someone on the beach.

"And?"

Eve gazed out to sea. "Maybe... maybe he'd been doing it for a while... keeping an eye on the place."

"Casing the joint?" Jill asked.

"And... and when he saw Alex arrive he realized he had his chance to frame me."

"Whoa. This is a new theory."

"Not really. All along I've felt as if someone tried to pin this on me. Except they didn't count on me having an alibi for the night."

"Just because you were with Helena doesn't mean you couldn't have killed Alex before you left. Forensics might provide a time of death, but I'm betting it'll be something like between four and seven o'clock."

"It's amazing how much you seem to know, Jill." Eve swung toward her. "Tell me again why you came to see me that night?" She watched Jill's lips press together. "Sorry, I'm doing it again. We're supposed to work together, not turn on each other."

Jill's face tensed and she lunged for her, clamping

her hands on Eve's shoulders, her fingers digging into her.

"What—"

For someone with a small frame Jill had quite a lot of speed and power. In one quick motion, she turned Eve around. Eve imagined she'd try to twist her arm around her throat. Losing her balance the way she had, Jill would have no trouble putting enough pressure to snap her neck. Instead, she pressed her hand hard over her mouth.

"Look." Jill's voice was a hard whisper against Eve's ear.

Eve's eyes were wide open, another second and her eyeballs would have popped out in shock. She looked and she tried to see. She couldn't speak because Jill's hand was still clamped over her mouth so she shook her head.

"Over there. The back door," Jill whispered, her hand easing off the pressure.

And then Eve saw the shape of a tall man racing along the side of the house. She gave a sharp nod.

Gradually, Jill released her hold.

Moments later Eve crouched down. She leaned against a rock and rubbed her neck. "Ouch."

"Are you all right?"

"Still in shock."

"Sorry. It was a knee-jerk reaction. I caught sight of

the movement and I wanted you to look and shut up at the same time."

"A simple, hey Eve, look over there, would have sufficed."

"Don't you realize sound travels over water?"

"Still water. This is the sea. And... where did you learn those moves?" Eve asked.

"Self defense classes. My parents insisted." Jill gave a lift of her shoulders. "Sometimes I don't know my own strength."

Eve groaned. "I think I might have to wear a neck brace."

"So, who do you think that was?"

"I only saw the shape of a man. I think he was wearing a cap, but I can't be sure. He was tall... as tall as..." She didn't want to say it. So far, she had thought of everyone as a suspect.

"Richard Parkmore?"

"Maybe."

"Now what? Do we keep going this way up to the house or call the police?"

"We'll check the house first." Although she was in no hurry to do that. If nothing had been taken then that meant her visitor had come for her. "Come on, there are only a few more rocks to climb over."

"Hey, wait," Jill called out.

"Quit grumbling and keep up." Eve turned and saw

Jill bend down, her hand reaching for something behind a rock.

"Eve."

"You don't have to shout. I'm right here. What did you find?"

Jill held up what looked to be a phone. "Do you think this is it?"

"The case is cracked."

"That doesn't matter. The card should still be fine." Jill waved the phone. "Do you realize what this means?"

"I think you might have just blown the case wide open. Whatever information we can retrieve from it will lead us straight to..."

"Richard Parkmore," Jill said. "It has to belong to him."

"Yes, probably. But we can't be sure. The man had no more use for his phone and threw it away. Okay, that was bad. He should have waited until he found a trash-can. He should be fined for littering. But can we really start thinking of him as a killer?"

"Better him than me," Jill said in a huff.

Chapter Thirteen

"I DON'T LIKE this at all," Jill complained.

"Where's your youthful spirit of adventure?"

"I left it back at your place. More specifically, back at the beach where we saw that man coming out of your place. It's all been used up now."

"You still don't want to be seen with me? Too bad," Eve said.

"Too bad? As in, if you go down, you'll take me down with you?"

"You're being overly dramatic."

"Am I? Think about it. Someone's after you. They see me with you. Soon enough, they'll figure out you're staying at my place. What if they come after you there, do away with you and then kill me too? They're not likely to leave me behind as a witness." Jill shook her head. "Be honest, do you really want to be out and about on a night like this?"

"We have to eat and I'm feeling too jittery to cook and that's saying a lot because cooking usually calms me down." After checking the house, Eve had insisted they drive into town for dinner. There hadn't been anything missing in the house. That meant she had been the target. "Anyway, the danger's passed. I'm sure of it."

Jill chortled. "So, you had a lucky escape. Great, you live to tell the tale."

"Again with that menacing tone. You remind me of Puss in Boots. All sweetness one moment and then the claws come out."

"I'm cranky. I'm missing my favorite show."

"You sound like a teenager with a short attention span. Whatever happened to solving the mystery?"

"Is that what we're supposed to be doing? I thought the police were handling that. And, for the record, I'm here with you under duress."

"Well, the police are taking too long. Clearly, they need help." Eve made a point of driving past the squad car parked on the main street a couple of times before finally finding a parking space.

"Whatever happened to you coming to the island to relax?"

"There's no chance of me doing that now. The killer has seen to that."

"You could at least try," Jill said. "Rise above your circumstances."

"How do you suggest I do that? Change the subject? Discuss the weather? Take up knitting?"

"Have you read Mira's latest novel?" Jill asked. "Her books suck you right in. You could try losing yourself in reading."

Eve dipped her head in embarrassment. The last time she'd tried to lose herself in one of Mira's books, she'd fallen asleep. All those boy meets girl and hits it off but decides it's not a good idea to get mixed up in a relationship stories always had her rolling her eyes. Why start a conversation with someone, get them all hot and bothered, if you were going to find an excuse not to follow through?

Eve cleared her throat. "You know I can never go home again. Not until this sordid business is finally wrapped up."

"My house is your house. But I'm still not happy about you making me a sitting target by association."

Eve parked the car and they strode off in search of a place to have dinner. "I'm thinking I should pack up and leave now. Go back to New York."

"What makes you think you'll be safe there," Jill said and twirled an imaginary evil villain mustache.

"Please stop doing that."

"I will if we can share a pizza." Jill didn't wait for her to answer and instead gave her a tug toward the island's only pizza place. Eve went willingly because it carried a full menu of mostly Italian dishes and she needed something hearty to keep her going.

They sat at the only available table, which happened to be by the window. A bad idea, Eve thought since she could be seen from the street. She shook off the thought and switched her attention to the menu.

"Stop looking at the pasta. They make the best pizza in the world here."

"No one's stopping you from having some."

"That's just it. I can't stop at having some. If I order a small one, I'm always left wanting more. But if we share a large one, I can have half and a bit more. Come on, you owe me."

"I get the feeling I'm going to be paying for dragging you along for the rest of my stay on the island." She scanned the menu but before she could make an alternative suggestion, Jill placed their order. "Pizza with the lot?"

"You can pick out the bits you don't like. I suppose you're used to gourmet pizza with things like pesto and ricotta cheese."

"And sun dried tomatoes," Eve agreed. "You should try it. Variety is as good as a vacation."

Jill shrugged. "I'm attached to my predictability. There's nothing wrong with being humdrum."

"I'm sure the artist in you just shrunk back in horror."

When their pizza arrived, Eve discovered she was actually quite hungry and happy to focus on just eating. However, as they ate quietly, she noticed several glances shot her way.

"What do you suppose they're saying about me?"

Jill looked around them and smiled. "They're probably taking note of as many details about you as they can. I'm sure I saw someone taking a photo of you... in case they're interrogated by the police."

"It's good to have a sense of humor. Serves a purpose in time of need. But I'm not sure I like it when it's at my expense."

Jill finished the last of her pizza and they ordered some coffee. "Are we going to talk about the phone?"

"Not so loud," Eve warned.

"It's evidence, Eve. You have to turn it in. The sooner, the better."

"It can wait until tomorrow, what do you think the police will do with it tonight? They'll tag it and just dump it in an evidence locker and probably not get around to doing something about it until it's too late."

"Eve, what are you thinking?"

"Please don't take that tone with me. I'm not a

complete idiot. I'll hand it over... after we see if we can find anything. Who knows, the phone might still work."

"I'm not comfortable with this."

"That's because you already have a police record. What's the worst that can happen? Are you afraid of being charged as an accomplice?"

"It's all right for you. You'll have your fun and then leave, but I have to stay on. I like my life nice and quiet. At this rate, I'm going to have fingers pointed at me, and accusations of hanging out with the wrong type made."

Eve laughed. "I've never been thought of as a bad influence. Okay, how about we go back to your place and watch a film on TV. There's bound to be something on. Get our minds off this business."

"Before or after we pull the phone apart?"

"Well, that was disappointing," Jill said and grabbing a cushion, curled up on the couch.

"I'd been hoping for a better result," Eve agreed and set the phone down. "I guess I'll have to turn it over to the police after all."

"And get an earful while you're at it. Detective Yummy is not going to be pleased about you poking around and withholding evidence."

"He won't know I've been poking around."

"So, you just happened to find the phone on one of your walks?'

"I could slip it into an envelope and drop it off at the precinct. That way I remain anonymous. Do you have any more chocolate chip cookies?"

"You've already eaten a bagful."

"Brain food."

"More like sugar rush and you don't need more of that." Jill grumbled. "I thought you were giving it all a rest."

"I am but I still need to think." She yawned and getting up from the couch where they'd both collapsed when they'd returned to Jill's place, she strode over to the window. "The police are still out there." It was actually a comfort to know they'd been followed back to Jill's place. If anything happened and they yelled, none of the neighbors would hear them. The houses sat on large properties, some separated even further by patches of wilderness.

"Milk and cookies," Jill said as she set a tray down on the coffee table. "You're looking thoughtful. Stop it." She threw another log in the fire and gave Mischief and Mr. Magoo a scratch behind their ears.

"I can't. Any thoughts on who might have been coming out of Mira's house?"

"Someone tall, and definitely a man. Let's drop the subject now."

"Maybe the same someone who threw the phone over the cliff?"

"I thought you'd given up on making that connection. Talking about it back at the beach was one thing, now I'm going to toss and turn all night and I'll never be able to look at Richard Parkmore and not want to run off in the opposite direction. You know what they say about mud sticking."

"I wish I could figure out what he might have been looking for?" She strode over to the couch and picked up a cookie to nibble on. "He... the hypothetical man... not Richard Parkmore. Okay, I actually meant Richard. I'm sure it was him slinking off."

"You're forgetting he reported a break-in at his place."

"That could have been a ruse to throw everyone off his scent. You know, a red herring. He said he thought he recognized me from somewhere and I can't put my finger on it, but the more I think about it, the more I'd have to agree with him."

"Manhattan is a big place."

"What if he was somehow connected with Alex?" Eve shot to her feet. "The last time I saw Jack, my mind went off on a tangent weaving a tale about Patrick killing Mira—"

"You said that in one breath without blinking."

"Mira is fine. She'll return my call in her own good time."

"How can you be sure?"

"I know my aunt." She refused to think anything bad had happened to her. "Anyway, what if Richard had been somehow connected with Alex. That would mean bad news because Alex was always getting mixed up in one scheme or other that never ended well. Anyway, Richard would have known how to get in touch with him and lure him to the island. By the way, that's the little story I'd spun about Patrick, not that I really think he'd be capable of murder or anything underhanded."

Jill shook her head. "That sounds too farfetched." She shrugged. "Square pegs and round holes."

"I need something to work with."

"Eve, you're not the police. You don't need anything."

Eve ignored her. "I've entertained thoughts about a crime of passion, an accidental one where Patrick declares himself to Mira and when he's scorned, he's overcome by a lover's rage—"

"A scorned lover's rage," Jill asserted.

"Yes." Eve dunked her cookie in the glass of milk. "We need to start looking at a bigger picture. You heard Richard claim he had money trouble. My ex, Alex, might have been the source of those troubles. He was very good at that. If Richard had in any way been embroiled with Alex—"

"That's it, I'm going to bed. Coming?"

Eve shook her head. "I want to finish my milk and do some thinking."

Jill clicked her fingers and her two Labradors jumped to their feet only to stop. "I think they want to stay and keep you company. If they nudge you, take them out for a bit. They'll have a sniff around the yard and do their business."

"Okay." Eve sighed. Maybe she really did need to give it all a rest. Let the dust settle.

A few minutes later, Mischief, the smaller of the two Labs, pressed his wet nose against her. "All right." She grabbed a jacket and let them out, folding her arms against the evening chill. "Don't go too far. Evil things are lurking out there." The full moon was on the wane but there was enough light to make out the surrounding bushes. Like Mira's house, Jill's place sat on the beach.

Eve listened to the gentle lapping of the waves and watched a lone seagull fly by.

What had Alex been thinking, making her his beneficiary?

Had he been trying to make up for his past misdemeanors? And why had he been trying to contact her? Their divorce hadn't exactly been amicable. She'd been furious with him for derailing her life just when she'd thought it would be smooth sailing all the way.

He'd called, but he hadn't spoken...

She imagined him trying to get in touch with her to explain and clear the air... to maybe apologize and then at the last minute deciding it would be best to speak with her face to face.

She let her thoughts hover in her mind, not grabbing hold of any of them. When she went back inside, she'd keep her mind focused on tidying up and brushing her teeth... anything mundane. One step at a time, she thought. She might even focus on counting her breaths. By then, she would have fallen asleep and in the morning, she might wake up refreshed with only thoughts about coffee and donuts, instead of suspects and their motives.

Mr. Magoo slumped beside her and sighed.

Eve looked up and around. Mischief was nowhere in sight.

Then she heard a light whimper.

Huffing, she strode off in the direction of the sound. It had come from the trail that meandered along the beach. Eve decided she wouldn't venture far, only to the edge of the clearing and call Mischief from there.

She picked up some rustling noises and some more whimpers. "Mischief. Come back, boy," she called out lightly, although she didn't really think the dog would obey. They'd only met a couple of times now. It would probably be presumptuous of her to think Jill's dogs would respond to her.

Mr. Magoo padded ahead of her and stopped to look back. "I'm right behind you. Lead the way, but I'm warning you, I'll only keep going if the path remains lit. No dragging me into the dark, please."

She looked over her shoulder to make sure the house remained in sight. Another whimper had her picking up her pace. Mr. Magoo trotted off only to again stop and check on her progress.

"Good boy. I'm coming." She stabbed the toe of her boot on a tree root and nearly stumbled. Keeping her eyes to the ground, she made her way, her steps cautious. The last thing she needed right then was to fall and twist her ankle. She doubted Jill would hear her. When she looked ahead and saw Mr. Magoo disappear around a bend, she picked up her pace.

"I think you two are having fun at my expense. Come back." A branch brushed against her face. Eve twirled around and swatted it. When she turned back, she took a step and made contact with a solid form. Her arms flailing, she tried to catch her balance by stretching her leg and leaping over the obstruction.

Mischief woofed.

"You could have warned me—" Her hands came up to her mouth.

Mischief woofed again.

Eve stumbled back then took a step forward to see what had nearly tripped her over.

Another body.

Chapter Fourteen

EVE GAZED up from her cup of hot cocoa. Detective Jack Bradford didn't look pleased. His mouth was set in a hard line, and his eyes had probably only blinked once in the last five minutes.

Someone had spread a blanket around Eve's shoulders and had thrown another log in the fire. She sat huddled on the couch, her feet tucked under her.

"Finished with your drink?" he asked.

She took another slurp. "Not quite." He'd been decent, giving her time to gather her composure.

Eve closed her eyes. Her head was still spinning.

After nearly tripping over the body, she'd sprinted back to the house, desperately searching her pockets for her cell phone, which she'd actually left behind in her handbag. When she'd reached the front door, she'd pushed herself off it and had sprinted off toward the road where she knew the squad car would still be parked.

She'd slammed against it, her hands pounding on the driver's window.

The officer had had to wind the window down to ask her to please step back so he could open the driver's door.

She'd been frantic and had struggled to catch her breath.

"Eve."

Her finger twitched then sprung up, calling for another minute.

Jack checked his watch then strode off to speak with one of the police officers standing by the door.

When he returned, he again sat opposite her.

Eve nodded. "Okay. What do you want to know?"

"I want you to tell me everything that happened tonight."

"Jill and I went to dinner—"

"I'm aware of that. I meant the moment you went outside. Why did you go outside?"

"Mischief," she took a sip of her drink.

"Yes, I know. I warned you to stay put."

"Mischief and Mr. Magoo, they're Jill's Labradors." She took another sip. "They needed to go out and Jill had gone to bed so I took them out... and..."

"And you felt compelled to go snooping around?"

"Hey, blame Mischief. He took off. What was I supposed to do? Call for backup?" She finished her drink but instead of setting the mug down, she held it against her and told Jack everything she could remember from the moment she'd stepped outside. "I didn't see anything to suggest there was something wrong, but then I heard Mischief's whimpering."

"And you didn't hear anything before that? No approaching footsteps?"

"If I had, I would have run out to the squad car straight away."

He nodded as if in approval. "Would you like another drink?"

"No, thank you." She gave the blanket a tug and drew it closer to her. "What's going to happen now? You know I didn't kill him."

Jack shook his head. "You didn't. Henry Parkmore is alive."

"Poor Henry." Her lips parted and she pushed out a sigh of relief. "I didn't stop to see who it was. I just ran. Then the police officer went to investigate, and soon after the ambulance arrived. I then heard the police officer reporting the incident and mentioning Henry's name." Another victim, she'd thought, and then she'd worried because the officer had guided her back inside the house. By then, a backup squad car had arrived and an officer had stood guard over her.

"So what happened to him? Did someone try to kill him too?"

"We won't know that for a while. Henry Parkmore hasn't regained consciousness."

But he was alive. If the death toll rose, and she had anything to do with it, she'd never be able to live with herself. Bad enough Alex had lost his life and she knew, without a doubt, that it had something to do with her. She was the only solid link to Alex. Sure, she'd been trying to connect Richard Parkmore to him... but that remained an assumption.

"Where was Jill while all this was happening?"

"She'd gone to bed." And she was still there. Eve couldn't believe she'd slept through all this. "What about Richard Parkmore? Have you spoken with him?"

"Yes. He's at the hospital now. He's very upset."

"Mmm."

"What?"

"He's supposed to be looking after Henry."

"He said Henry snuck out."

People didn't just sneak out to go wandering about in the middle of the night. They had to have a reason. She'd had a reason to step out...

"Whatever you're thinking, stop it," Jack warned.

"I can't help it. Why would Henry go out in the middle of the night? There has to be an explanation."

"Eve, let us do our job."

"And what am I supposed to do in the meantime?"

"Sit tight."

"Like a sitting duck?"

"The police are within easy reach. You'll be fine just so long as you don't go wandering off. No more walking along the tracks. Stick to the main road, better still, if you need to go somewhere, drive. The squad car will follow."

She shifted slightly. "Sorry to get you out here so late. I hope I didn't interrupt anything." The words spilled out before she could think better and hold them back.

"I was at the precinct doing some paper work."

"Oh. You keep very long hours." Did that mean he didn't have someone to go home to? "It's very comforting to know you're on the job."

He stood up. "Try and get some rest and stay indoors."

"I slept through all that?" Jill asked the next morning.

"It's a sign of a clear conscience."

"Are you saying what I think you're saying?"

Eve gave her a small smile. "Yes, for once you're in the clear."

"What about you?"

Eve bent down to give Mischief a scratch behind the ear. "Jack only wanted to know how I'd found Henry. Once I explained I'd gone chasing after Mischief, he seemed satisfied." She frowned. "Then again, there's a police officer posted outside the door, so they've stepped up their presence... which could mean they're more concerned about me... being a victim... or a murderer."

"Maybe he could give us an update on Henry Parkmore. I'll go and ask."

"I saw you peering out the window just before, Jill."

"And?"

"You have a thing for that young officer."

"So, what if I do?"

"If you do, then I suggest you do something about the smudge of chocolate on your chin."

"*Ooops*, thanks."

"Never say I don't have your back."

After clearing out the breakfast dishes, Eve had a long shower. She'd only brought a couple of changes of clothing with her, so some time during the day she'd have to think about going back to Mira's. But she was in no hurry.

Grabbing her phone, she slipped it into her back pocket and strode out to find Jill. Eve felt she was imposing on her time, so she'd have to figure out some way to keep herself busy while Jill worked on her painting or whatever she did during the day.

As she strode into the sitting room, she heard voices.

Jack and Jill.

She laughed.

"Look what the lovely detective brought us. Coffee."

"And donuts?" Eve asked.

"Of course," he said.

"Is this your way of suggesting we stay put and don't interfere with your investigation because nothing good can come of it?"

Jack smiled. "Thank you. You saved me the trouble of having to explain it to you."

Eve held up the coffee in a salute. "I wouldn't want you to walk away thinking I'm a troublemaker." The edge of his lip quirked up and Eve could imagine him thinking she wasn't a troublemaker, but rather... a trouble magnet.

"Any good news this morning?"

"Henry Parkmore is out of danger."

That was a relief. "Oh, come on. Is that all you have for us?"

"If I tell you more, will you promise you won't get a false sense of security?"

"Absolutely."

"This wasn't about an attempt on Henry's life."

"So, our killer had nothing to do with it?" She raked her fingers through her hair. "That sets my mind at ease. I hate to think the killer is stepping up his campaign of terror, but... how can you be sure?"

"Henry Parkmore has a history of illness. He suffered a mild stroke. Apparently, it's quite common with his condition. There's some disorientation involved. At the time, his speech would have been affected. Even now, he's not making much sense."

"He wasn't making sense when he was all right. I think Henry has been rambling for quite some time. Is he actually talking this morning?"

Jack nodded. "He expressed concern for Mira Lloyd. We assume she was on his mind when he set out last night."

"You think he was headed out to the house?"

Jack nodded. "Perhaps not for the first time. His nephew, Richard, said he often has to go chasing after him."

"So, it wasn't the killer striking again?" And the shadows she'd seen on her first night might have been Henry Parkmore wandering around.

"Eve, I told you. No false sense of security."

Did Henry have reason to be worried about Mira? She hated not knowing where she was... how she was. But she couldn't let herself be distracted by negative thoughts. "Are you stepping up your investigation?"

"We're still gathering evidence."

"I was thinking of returning to New York," she said testily.

"I wouldn't recommend that. In fact, it was very sensible of you to come stay with Jill."

"Do you hear that, Jill? That means you're officially off the suspect list." Eve set her cup down on the coffee table. "And me too. Otherwise, they wouldn't let me stay with you."

Jill took a step back, putting herself out of Jack's line of vision, and waved to Eve. When Eve gave a small shrug, Jill pressed her hand to her ear.

"Oh, that reminds me. I have something for you. It might be nothing, but then again, who am I to say?" She looked around but couldn't see the phone anywhere. Looking up at Jill she saw her pointing toward the kitchen. "Back in a sec." Eve returned shortly with the phone in her hand, worrying her lip and hoping Jack wouldn't make a big deal out of it. "Jill and I were out on a walk yesterday and we found this." She shrugged. "It might have washed ashore... or maybe someone threw it away thinking it would land in the sea. Anyhow, we found it by the rocks near Mira's house." She handed the phone over.

Jack removed a plastic bag from the inside pocket of his jacket and held it out for Eve. The phone went in and he tapped it against the palm of his hand, his eyebrows drawn down.

"I honestly wasn't out there looking for trouble."

"Just make sure it doesn't find you."

"So, do you think it'll be of any use to your investigation?"

"I'll hand it over to forensics. They'll know what to do with it."

"And then you'll let us know what you find?" she asked, her tone cheerful, somewhat hopeful and verging on mischievous.

"This is so strange. I can't remember the last time I had a whole day to myself with nothing to do." Eve watched Mr. Magoo zigzag his way ahead of them and then stop to see if they were following. "So, tell me about your daily schedule."

Jill sighed. "Walk the boys. Paint. Read. Paint. Walk the boys."

"What about a social life? Friends to visit?"

"I'm twenty-four. Everyone my age has moved on. They're all working in the city."

"What about Samantha over at the bookstore? She looks to be about your age."

"She is, but we never hung out together at school. I doubt we'd have anything in common."

"Have you tested the waters?"

"Are you trying to get rid of me?"

Mischief came up to them and barked or at least made a sound that sounded like a bark.

"What's wrong, boy? Are we going too slow for you?" Eve asked and hoped Mischief hadn't acquired a nose for finding bodies and now felt bereft because there were none around for him to sniff out.

"You know he doesn't talk human."

"Dogs are smart. They understand."

"Maybe you should get one," Jill suggested.

"I need to do some thinking first. There's no point in getting a puppy and then sticking it in a small apartment."

"You should stay on the island."

"Oh, yeah?" Just like that?

"Why not?"

"Plenty of reasons. It would feel too much like giving up. A part of me feels I should be out there, doing something, trying something new." They came up to Mira's house. "Okay. I'm going in to get a change of clothes and I'll meet you out here again." She watched Mischief and Mr. Magoo trot off down to the beach. "I think I can guess what you're going to do."

"I'll see you back here," Jill said and took off after her dogs.

Eve dug her keys out of her back pocket and let herself in through the back door. Sprinting up to her bedroom, she grabbed an old backpack out of the wardrobe and filled it up with essential items. Enough for a couple of days, she thought. Then she'd bring it all back and spend a day doing the laundry and airing the place out.

When she had everything she wanted, she went down to the kitchen and checked the refrigerator to see if she had to throw anything out.

Seeing Jill a fair distance away on the beach, she figured she had another twenty minutes wait so she made herself a coffee.

She stood by the window sipping it and thinking about Henry Parkmore. It was a relief to know he hadn't been attacked. How could Richard have let him out of his sight? She'd seen it happen the day after she'd arrived on the island when Henry had accosted her.

A thought occurred and she couldn't leave it alone.

It would have been convenient for everyone to think Henry had been attacked. It would definitely let Richard off the hook since no one would think him capable of attacking his own uncle.

A ruse.

Just like the break-in he'd reported at his house.

It's what she'd do if she wanted to draw the scent away from her.

When Jill returned, Eve decided they'd both go through all the bookshelves, and trawl their way from one end of the house to the other until they found something. Anything. Whoever had broken in, had been looking for something significant.

For a wild moment, she thought of Abby. Mira got all her books from her store. Was there a connection?

Eve laughed.

Okay, now she'd gone too far.

If she had to point the finger of blame at anyone, it would have to be...

Richard Parkmore.

Because?

He had money problems.

And how did one resolve money problems?

By stealing, of course.

From where she stood, she glanced over at the bookshelves. Mira's books were all paperbacks. She doubted her aunt had ever purchased a first edition.

Mira.

Where are you?

One more day, she thought and she'd have to turn the house upside down looking for Mira's personal information. If she had her banking details, she could contact them and see if they could provide information about credit card activity. She only needed some peace of mind. A part of her insisted Mira was still sorting stuff out and would return in her own good time.

Thinking about it, she realized Mira had actually done a disappearing act a couple of times before, with Eve only finding out after the event but not always. In fact, she couldn't remember Mira mentioning her trip to Pennsylvania. The Amish quilts on her bed looked new. One of them even had layers of tissue paper still in it.

Mira practiced such intense focus while she wrote but in other areas, she could be quite forgetful to the point of being indifferent, never really worrying or thinking anything bad was going to happen. In fact, Eve would bet anything that once she called, she'd be dismissive of any feeling of concern.

It still wouldn't stop her from giving her aunt a piece of her mind. Of course, Mira would merely give her one of her blank expressions and shuffle off to do some writing.

She chuckled under her breath.

She was about to turn away from the window to wash the mug when she stopped.

The house almost felt too still.

Too quiet.

She held her breath.

And then she heard it.

The slightest noise. The creak of a door.

She set the mug down, and edged her way toward the sitting room, even as her instinct told her to run out the back door.

Someone was in the house.

All that time she'd been rummaging upstairs and while she'd been drinking her coffee, there had been someone in the house. She couldn't shake off the feeling.

Self-preservation urged her to retreat. Slowly and without alerting the intruder.

It wouldn't hurt to play it safe. Jill might laugh at her afterwards, but at least Eve would be alive to hear it.

Still holding her breath, she took a step back and another.

She figured she had about ten steps to take before she reached the back door. Eve kept her eyes on the sitting room entrance, praying that whoever was in there would stay put long enough for her to make her getaway.

She took another step just as her cell phone beeped a message.

Eve froze for a moment.

The door she'd heard creaking was slammed open and hurried steps made their way toward her.

She felt her body shake.

Somehow, she managed to tell herself to move.

And scream.

Yes, screaming would be good.

Screaming would raise the alarm, but she was too busy trying to move.

Clutching the phone against her chest, Eve swirled away and lunged for the back door just as a large hand curled around her arm.

Chapter Fifteen

EVE SCREAMED.

Not out of fear, but rather as a reaction, which was much the same thing.

It deafened her ears so it had to have caused some damage to the man trying to grab a hold of her.

She kicked. She pushed.

She rammed her elbow as hard as she could and connected with his ribcage.

All the while, Eve could hear the scuffling of their feet.

Neither one spoke.

Both breathed heavily.

Sheer anger and frustration took over.

She'd come to this island to relax.

Damn it.

She'd come to find peace and quiet.

Eve's rage worked its way up to her throat and she roared.

She tried to twist around and see his face, but his grip tightened and he pushed her toward the door, pressing her face against it.

All those shows she'd watched on late night television, surely something must have stuck, she thought and decided to quit struggling and go limp.

It seemed to work.

The man took a moment to adjust his grip and that's when she dug deep and found a strength she hadn't known she possessed.

She leaned forward and used the motion to propel herself back, blindly lifting her head and praying it would connect with the man's jaw.

Her prayers were answered.

He let out a yelp.

Eve hoped he'd bitten off his tongue.

In that split second, she managed to break free and wrench the back door open.

She didn't think she'd get more than three seconds grace to make her escape so she threw everything she had into it and then some, pushing her legs to pump harder until she could feel every muscle in her body screaming with pain.

Acting so quickly, she didn't have time to pick a direction.

Instinct told her to aim for open space and that meant the beach, but Jill was there and Eve didn't want to draw her into danger so she headed in the opposite direction, toward the front of the house, hoping to reach the road ahead of her pursuer.

Taking the corner like a motorcycle at a grand prix, she then straightened and leaned forward hoping that would add speed to her frantic steps.

When she looked up, she saw him appear.

They both came to a screeching halt.

He'd come out the front of the house.

He...

Richard Parkmore.

His face was contorted with rage, his teeth gritting and Eve thought she saw blood trailing along his chin.

Eve took a second to consider her options again.

If she ran along the path and headed toward Jill's place, she'd eventually be able to call for help. Surely the police there would hear her. But it all depended on her speed. Did she have it in her to outrun him?

He was taller and she didn't think he looked that fit. She wanted to believe she had an advantage. She had years of training, years of standing on her feet and hauling large pots and pans around.

She didn't have a choice.

She had to go for it.

She ran.

Do not, whatever you do, look over your shoulder, she told herself.

Every time she'd seen someone in a movie running from danger, they'd looked over their shoulders and that always slowed them down enough to get caught. So, she decided to focus her gaze on a point just ahead of her.

The path was too narrow to do any maneuvering. Otherwise she would have used Mr. Magoo's tactics and zigzagged her way along.

Behind her, she heard Richard growl.

With her head start, she'd put several bodies' distance between them and she had no intention of losing ground. Not to a killer.

Just then her phone rang.

With so much panic surging through her veins, she couldn't think. Her lungs were beginning to burn. She could hear the pounding of his footsteps and thought he might have gained some ground but she refused to turn around to look.

Argh. She wanted to yell her frustration. Her arms were pumping just as hard as her legs. She tried to focus and coordinate her body. Damn it. She was a woman. She could multitask. Her phone continued to ring. She only needed to press one button.

Risking everything, she brought her hand up and looked at the phone long enough to guide her finger to the correct button, but just then she felt a tug.

Richard Parkmore's fingertips had connected with her sweater. She went ahead and pressed the button and prayed she'd hit the right one.

Eve lost her balance and stumbled but then straightened. Her steps were awkward but her legs kept moving.

He roared again. Eve imagined him foaming at the mouth.

Another tug.

"Help," she screamed. She had no idea if she'd succeeded in hitting the right button but she didn't dare check. She could only hope the person who'd rung was still on the line.

When she saw the clearing coming up, she panicked.

If Richard caught up with her then, they'd be close to the cliff and that was one place she didn't want to be in.

She screamed again but when she did, she lost her rhythm. Again, he reached for her. She knew this because this time he managed to push her.

Her arms flapped about and she desperately tried to keep herself upright. And that's when she collided with a solid shape.

At first, Eve thought she'd crashed against a tree trunk.

But then a strong set of arms hauled her to the side as if she weighed nothing more than rag doll. One moment she'd been running, and the next she found herself sitting on her butt staring up at Jack who had his back to her.

In front of them both was Richard Parkmore crouching and looking like a cornered animal.

Clearly, he'd lost his senses because he actually lunged for her, the noise emanating from his bloodied mouth making him sound like a raving lunatic.

Jack had him pinned to the ground in two easy moves.

Eve blew her hair out of her eyes and snorted.

She'd seen that move plenty of times. Why hadn't she thought of doing it?

Jack looked over his shoulder at her. "Are you all right?"

She nodded.

His gaze skated over her body as if looking for something she might have missed.

"I'm all right," she insisted, speaking around her choppy breaths.

He gave a nod and turned back to Richard. Taking his foot off his back, he pulled his hands together and handcuffed him.

She held her hand against her chest. Her heart still pounded. She counted to five. "Jack?"

"Yes?"

"Was that you on the phone... calling me?"

"Yes." The edge of his lip kicked up. "Do you always answer your phone with a scream for help?"

Only when she was running for her life.

"I think I've lost part of my hearing."

"So what did you want?" she asked.

"To remind you to stay put."

Collapsing on her back, Eve stared up at the sky.

"You ruined everything."

She slanted her eyes toward Richard Parkmore and quickly looked away. She didn't want the image imprinted in her mind in case it came back to haunt her.

"Yeah, tell that to the judge." Sure, she was curious and wanted to know the full story but she'd just scraped through with her life in one piece, and all she could think about was lying back and gazing up at the sky... and catching her breath. The sky looked so calm and so far removed from the troubles down below; it somehow put everything into perspective.

She relaxed her face and smiled, a small sigh pushing past her lips.

Remembering the phone message that had prompted Richard to make his move, Eve used what little energy she had left, raised her hand and brought her phone to eye level.

She tapped the screen and found the last message.

"Mira." With a grunt, Eve sprung upright and tried to focus on the words.

Coming home. Hope to still find you there.

She heard Jack read Richard Parkmore the Miranda rights to which Richard answered with another litany of growls.

He was actually foaming at the mouth, or at least spitting.

Unfortunately, he'd opted to remain otherwise silent.

Eve supposed that put her at Jack's mercy. He'd either share what he would eventually extract from Richard or he'd make her wait until she could read all about it in the newspapers.

"Hey, Richard. Has anyone ever told you that you run like a girl?" she asked.

Again, he told her she'd ruined everything.

"Oh, poor baby," she couldn't help taunting him.

"You found it, didn't you?" he spat out.

She shrugged. "What can I say, intuition is a woman's natural talent." Although, she had no idea what he meant.

"If Henry hadn't written that letter, your aunt would never have found out my plans and she would never have contacted Alex."

So, there was a letter and presumably, Richard had been trying to find it, hence the break-in. And she didn't have to hear him confess to that. It had been Richard...

It sounded as if she and Mira would have plenty to talk about when she returned. Eve bit the edge of her lip. Mira had contacted Alex... and whatever had been in that letter had prompted Alex into action. "Well, she did."

"I never thought Alex had it in him to come to your rescue."

Her rescue? What had Richard Parkmore been planning? "Alex was many things, but never a coward." A thieving weasel, but not a coward, she insisted.

"It'll be Henry's word against mine. He's a rambling old fool."

"It was very nice of your uncle to put it all in writing," she reminded him.

He roared again and made a futile effort to break free of his handcuffs.

"Did you really think you'd get away with it?" she asked. She had no idea what had been written, but the question was generic enough to bait him into hopefully revealing more.

"I would have. I'm just as good as Alex, if not better. You would have fallen for me eventually. Mira Lloyd's going to leave you her fortune. A chance to marry an heiress doesn't come along every day—" He seemed to realize then he'd said too much.

But enough for Eve to start putting some pieces together.

Marry him?

To fix his money problems?

She couldn't help laughing under her breath. Marry another man like Alex and fall for the same trap? Not in this lifetime.

The police arrived then and took Richard away.

Jack stretched his hand down to her.

"I'm still catching my breath." And doing a quick mental review of the last few days. She'd never experienced such an adrenaline rush in her life.

Marry Richard?

How had she ruined it all? By coming back to the house and finding him? If she hadn't, then eventually, the case might have been filed away unsolved. That would have left Richard free to pursue her.

But she'd ruined it all. By finding Richard in the house? Proof that he'd been the one who'd broken in.

Eve gave herself a mental pat on the back. "Okay. I'm ready."

Jack took hold of her hand and helped her up. "Can you walk?"

"In my mind, I think I'm still running." She

wondered what would happen if she went limp. Would Jack gather her in his arms and pick her up?

Eve's lips parted then her mouth gaped open.

That was something she'd never be able to mention to Mira.

"Mira sent me a message. She's on her way home," she said.

"That's a relief."

"How did you get here so fast?" It occurred to ask.

"I was already at Jill's house. The phone you gave us provided a solid lead. I came to make sure you were staying put. I'd already sent the police over to Richard's place to arrest him."

A feeling of warmth uncurled inside her. He could have just sent the officer over to her, but he hadn't.

"So the phone belonged to Richard."

Jack nodded.

"He'd been in contact with your ex. But the calls stopped a week before you arrived."

"I guess we won't be able to fill in all the gaps until we read the letter."

"We?"

Eve huffed out a breath. "Even if you confiscate the letter, Mira will still be able to tell me what was in it, so there's no point in trying to leave me out of the loop." She looked up at him. "Jack, you wouldn't... would you?"

Not surprisingly, he didn't answer.

They strode back to Jill's house and found her there.

When she spotted Eve, she ran toward her.

"You're all right. You're all right," she kept saying. Then a barrage of words spilled out, tripping over each other. "I was walking along the beach, then I turned and thought I saw you run out of the house. Actually, Mr. Magoo spotted you first. We all ran back, but by the time I got there you'd disappeared. I ran onto the road to see if there was still a squad car parked outside your place and there was. They called it in and brought us back here. I've been frantic. The dogs haven't stopped pacing."

She looked down at both Mr. Magoo and Mischief. Their tails had turned into propellers, they were that happy.

"I saw them take Richard Parkmore away. What happened?" Jill asked.

"Oh, we went for a bit of a run."

"Eve."

"He was skulking around the house. Actually, he was in the house. All that time I was in there," she shivered. "He must have been looking for the letter."

"What letter?"

"Henry Parkmore wrote Mira a letter. We don't know what was in it, but... there must have been some mention of Richard's plan to marry me."

"Marry you?"

Eve grinned and fluttered her eyelashes. "Henry must have disapproved of Richard's plans. And we know Henry has been rambling, so maybe he rambled on about it to Mira. He's very possessive of her, actually, he appears to be protective." Eve slanted her gaze at Jack who stood beside her, his hands hitched on his hips as he studied her. "We'll only know for sure when Mira returns... oh, I didn't tell you, Mira sent me a message. She's coming back. We have no idea where she's been but I'm going to hazard a guess and say she went to see Alex."

"Let's not get ahead of ourselves," Jack said.

"That's right. We need facts."

His eyebrow lifted.

Eve ignored the gesture. "It all comes down to Richard wanting to marry an heiress."

"Who?" Jill asked.

"Me, apparently." Eve raked her fingers through her hair. "I could really do with a long soak in your bathtub." She looked at Jack. "Unless you have any further questions you'd like to ask me?"

"They can wait until tomorrow."

The case was nowhere near closed, Eve thought.

Chapter Sixteen

EVE WANTED to get an early start to the day, so she could get to Mira's house and open some windows to air out the place before Mira returned.

She'd tried calling her aunt, but Mira was clearly avoiding talking on the phone which could only mean she was on the road driving.

Reluctant to miss out on anything or even stay alone in her house, Jill came along.

"I've never walked so much in my entire life. Or spent so much time thinking," Eve said.

"I've been going over what you told me Richard revealed yesterday, about Alex coming to your rescue. What do you think that was about?"

"I can only take a wild stab and say Richard had told Alex of his plans to woo me."

"Woo you?" Jill burst out laughing.

"They knew each other, that has to be a given now. I'm guessing Richard found out about the divorce and because he knew Alex, he must have also found out Mira was my aunt. Maybe Alex made a passing remark about missing out on the big prize. Seeing his chance, knowing his uncle lived on the island, Richard might have decided to gain some sort of advantage. I'm thinking he planned on taking his time."

"Wooing you?"

"Why not?"

"You somehow don't strike me as the type to respond to that sort of attention or fall in love."

"For your information, I loved Alex. Divorcing him wasn't easy." She then remembered her first encounter with Richard. There had been something... a sort of eagerness about him. She shrugged it all off, thinking they'd get the facts after Jack drilled Richard for them.

They came up to the house and let themselves in through the back door.

Striding into the sitting room, they both stopped.

Mira sat on the couch drinking a cup of tea and nibbling on a muffin. Eve couldn't remember her ever looking so good. Dressed in a stylish pair of dark gray pants and a light pink sweater with a polo neck, her graying hair had been cut into a short bob; a new look for Mira who'd always worn her hair in a thick braid.

In an instant, Eve forgot all about telling Mira off for leaving without saying anything.

She yelped. "Mira!" Eve threw herself at her aunt and was surprised to find her eyes tearing up. "You have no idea what's been happening here."

"I think I do. Hello, Jill."

Jill hesitated, and then she too rushed to Mira and threw her arms around her.

"I've never felt so popular."

"When did you get back?" Eve asked. "We've been so worried about you."

"Really?" Mira sighed. "I suppose I'll have to go through the whole sorry tale again."

"What do you mean again?"

"I've just spent an hour at the precinct talking to Detective Jack Bradford. Have you met him?"

"Yes... but how did you know to go there?"

Another sigh. "Well, you know I don't watch the news or read newspapers. As I was driving back—"

"From?"

"From going to visit you, of course."

"You went to New York."

"I had to. Anyway, I heard the horrible news on the radio. I'd been looking for a music station when I heard Alex's name mentioned. I thought it best to drive straight to the precinct and tell them what I knew."

Eve sat up. "You better start from the beginning. We know there was a letter."

"Yes, Henry Parkmore wrote it. That's the reason why I had to warn you his nephew was keeping an eye out for your next visit and if he was anything like Henry, he would have been unrelenting in his pursuit of you. When I didn't find you, I contacted Alex. It never occurred to think you'd come here. And your neighbors weren't at all helpful."

"You drove all that way, just to see me and warn me—"

"Oh, there was also a planned visit to my publisher. They'd been badgering me to do some promotional work for some time now and had organized a book signing." She took a sip of her tea. "I never even suspected it would all turn out the way it did. If I'd known Richard Parkmore could be so dangerous, I would have..." Mira shook her head, "Well, I couldn't go to the police then because I had nothing to go on with. There's no law preventing a man from deciding he'll pursue a woman with the intention of marrying her."

"But Alex must have known something could happen. Otherwise why come all this way..." To face his death.

"I suppose so," Mira said. "But Alex only came after I spoke with him. I wanted to find out more about Richard Parkmore's background. People come to the island and they try to blend in so we don't know what's gone on in their lives beforehand."

Eve shook her head. "I can't begin to tell you how I feel about Alex putting himself in harm's way just because he felt compelled to warn me."

Mira chuckled lightly. "If it's any help, Alex was fuming. The thought of someone else jumping in and grabbing what he hadn't been able to, made him see red."

"He can't have been that bad. He included me in his will."

Mira patted her hand. "Yes, as a way to show you he meant business. He wanted to get you back for himself. Over my dead body, he said after I showed him the letter Henry had sent me."

"That's the part I don't get," Jill said. "Why would Henry explain it all to you in a letter?"

"Oh, he rambled a lot. His thoughts came and went. It's all a shame. He used to have such a sharp mind. Henry used to be my financial advisor. Then he retired and came to live on the island. It didn't take me long to realize he had a protective way about him. All those years looking after my finances and then the onslaught of his illness left him so confused." Mira sighed.

"I wouldn't mind reading the letter," Eve said.

"Sorry, I had to turn it in as evidence."

Eve slumped back and brushed her hands across her

face. "I'm glad you went away. Just think, what if you'd confronted Richard and he lost his temper with you."

"He was a bad apple. Henry complained about him not being any good with money and always living above his means. He said Richard had been pestering him about his big plans and how he'd strike it lucky, and that's why Henry wrote to me. I'm just glad he found a moment of clarity to put it all down on paper and not try to tell me himself. He could rattle on and lose his way."

Eve shook her head. "Richard had the nerve to say I'd ruined everything."

"He was the type to blame everyone else for his misfortunes, never accepting responsibility for his actions."

Eve didn't want to admit it, but two men had fought over her, and they'd both come out losers. Two wrongs definitely didn't make a right.

Or did it?

Eve thought about Jack Bradford...

Best to keep her mind on finding something worthwhile to do and well away from any romantic involvement, she thought.

"You know you saved Henry Parkmore," Mira said.

"How do you figure that?" Eve asked.

"That nice detective filled me in on what happened. If you hadn't found him that night, then I doubt he would have survived the night outdoors."

It had been an accident. If she hadn't taken the dogs out, Mischief would never have picked up Henry's scent and she would not have gone chasing after Mischief...

"So, what will happen to Henry now?"

"Henry will spend his days in a convalescing home. I'm sure he'll drive everyone nuts, but I like to think he'll finally find someone there. He'll fall in love—"

"Oh, Mira. Do you really think there's someone for everyone?"

Mira laughed lightly and nodded. "And some people are lucky to find more than one special someone."

"Please don't look at me when you say that."

"You're too young to be cynical." Mira rose to her feet. "I have some unpacking to do."

"Hang on. What did you think of Jack Bradford?" Eve couldn't help asking.

"I liked him so much, I'm thinking of putting him in my next novel. A swashbuckling pirate who inherits a dukedom."

"Oh, I can't wait to read that one," Jill said.

Mira slanted her gaze toward Eve.

Eve looked away coyly. "I'll give it a go. But you know I'm not a big reader." She surged to her feet. "I was going to prepare you a feast but I haven't had the chance to shop. How about we all go out to lunch. Jill? Do you feel safe enough to be seen with me?"

"What's that about? Why wouldn't Jill feel safe?" Mira asked.

"Oh, nothing much. Just that for a while there, we'd all become suspects in an ongoing murder investigation. Now that I think of it, no one suspected you, Mira. And you would have been an ideal candidate. Pretending to be missing and all the while lurking in the shadows and emerging long enough to kill people."

"You had a lucky escape, Mira," Jill murmured.

"I take it you didn't?" Mira asked.

"What are you two talking about?"

"Nothing, dear. How about you both help me with the unpacking and then we can all go to lunch?"

"That sounds like a perfect plan."

Epilogue

A WEEK LATER, Eve sat on the front veranda with Mira.

A week of finally breathing easy and relaxing.

"It's been wonderful having you here." Mira raised her teacup to her lips. "Have you given any thought to extending your stay?"

"Well, I'm in no hurry to get cracking with my next project because I have no idea what it'll be. When I first arrived, I felt as if I had this deadline hanging over me and I had to make a quick decision, but the fact is, I can afford to take it easy for a couple of months."

"That's good to hear. Does that mean you're happy to relax here?" Mira asked.

"If you'll have me, yes."

"You know this is your home. The door is always open to you."

"You've no idea how good that makes me feel."

Mira's home had always been the one place where she felt safe, wanted and appreciated for herself.

A seagull hovered in the light breeze, squawked and flew away.

"I noticed Tinkerbelle's Bookshop is up for sale. You could buy it," Mira suggested in her usual no-nonsense manner.

"The thought occurred to me but I wouldn't be any good at it. People would want book recommendations and I wouldn't know where to start." She lifted her shoulder. "Something will come up."

"Then I might buy it as an investment. We wouldn't want a chain store to take it over and strip it of its uniqueness."

"That'll make Abby happy. She's keen to move on and expand her opportunities to meet someone. And of course, Samantha. I think she loves working there."

"Well, she could be in line for a promotion. Store Manager." Mira drained her cup and set it down. "You know I'm going away on one of my cruises."

"Yes, Helena Flanders mentioned it."

"I always feel uneasy about leaving the house empty. Do you think... maybe you'd want to stay and look after it?"

Eve smiled. "I'd love to." Eve wanted to mention the inheritance Richard Parkmore had been so fixated with, but that meant thinking about Mira no longer being around, so she didn't say anything.

"Oh, look," Mira said, "We have a visitor. Or at least you do."

Eve looked up.

Jack Bradford.

"He's probably here on official business."

"You can't be sure of that. I don't see him holding any official documents."

"He doesn't need documents to be official." He'd said he was always on official business. So, she had no business thinking he'd find another reason to come by.

"Well, we're about to find out. Despite what you say about my matchmaking ways, my money is on him coming here to see you."

Eve's gaze swept around his face taking in the square jaw, the firm mouth, then it drifted down to his broad shoulders. When her gaze dropped further, she could barely keep her eyes away from his narrow hips as he swaggered up the drive toward them. His jeans looked well-worn and hung low on his hips. His plain dark blue shirt was unbuttoned at the neck. His arms swung lightly beside him, but not in a carefree way. There was more purpose to his movements. Maybe he was here on official business after all...

"Hello, detective."

"Eve. Mira. How are you?"

"We're very well, thank you. We were both wondering what might have brought you out here..." Eve told herself to shut up, but she couldn't, "I told Mira you're always on official business, but the case has already been wrapped up, or so we hear."

He nodded and came up the steps.

"Have a seat." She focused on taking five breaths before offering him some coffee.

Deciding it would be safe to leave him with Mira, she trotted off to the kitchen. On the way back, she checked her reflection in the hallway mirror.

Okay, that definitely had to be a sign she was on the mend.

When she stepped out onto the veranda, Mira excused herself saying she'd had a spark of an idea for one of her books she needed to jot down.

"I have some cookies. I've spent the last couple of days baking up a storm for Mira. She loves to nibble on something while she writes."

"She's very lucky to have you." He took one and bit off the edge.

"I think so, yes."

"Any idea how long her luck is likely to run?"

She actually had to think about what he'd said before it clicked. "Oh, I haven't decided yet. Although, I have actually decided to take a break and not stress about having to make a decision straight away."

"That's a lot of decision making."

"I'm in no hurry. How about you? I suppose you have a lot of paperwork to catch up on and don't necessarily want to be rushed to your next crime scene."

"That's one place I'm never in a hurry to get to."

"But you do get there promptly." And thank goodness for that, she thought, not even wanting to imagine what would have happened if Jack hadn't arrived in the nick of time to save her from Richard' clutches.

"I assume you got a full confession from Richard Parkmore."

"He's been booked."

"You know I suspected him all along."

He laughed. "You'd say that."

"He had that preppy look about him that reminded me of Alex. It's a particular type I'm trying to avoid."

Jack looked down at himself.

"Oh, you don't have to worry. There's nothing preppy about you." Jack was the complete opposite, with that rugged, comfortable anywhere but in particular the outdoors, look. Eve had a sudden mental image of Jack chopping wood... bare-chested... looking up at her and smiling... raking his fingers through his thick hair... striding toward her.

"I'm glad to hear you say so. I'd hate to think you wouldn't be comfortable being seen out in public with me."

"In public? Where?"

"Somewhere like a restaurant."

"Are you asking me out to dinner, Jack?"

"Yes, I am. Would you have dinner with me, Eve?"

"How could I say no? It'll be interesting to see what else we have to talk about."

"I've been doing some reading."

Eve shifted in her seat. "Reading?"

"I was curious about Mira's books."

"Oh." She'd have to find out which one so she could read it too.

He laughed under his breath. "I guess I just came across as too eager to please."

He'd read a book... to please her? "Did you enjoy it?"

"Did I happen to mention I was eager to please?"

"Top marks for trying. Don't worry, we'll find some common ground. We can always talk about food. I know all about that."

He took another bite of his cookie. "There's a complexity of flavors to enjoy here."

"See, we're off to a great start."

Would you like to receive new release notifications?
Follow Sonia Parin on BookBub
Amazon page

Snuffed Out (Book 2 A Deadline Cozy Mystery) –
Scroll down to read Chapter One

Snuffed Out - Preview

CHAPTER ONE

"I'M dead on my feet. Honestly, whose idea was it to walk all the way into town? It doesn't feel so far when you're driving." Eve Lloyd flipped the menu over and continued her search for a tantalizing treat. There had to be some sort of reward for her efforts, and she'd decided she needed to put some in.

She'd been baking up a storm for her aunt Mira, a.k.a. renowned historical romance author, Elizabeth Lloyd, who loved to nibble on a cookie or two while writing. And Eve liked nothing better than cooking for her. However, cooking and tasting went hand in hand and it was beginning to pile up on her.

There weren't any significant changes to her waist-line... Yet. It had been a few months since she'd sold her restaurant and while her first attempt to relax had been sabotaged by a murder on the island, she'd eventually fallen in step with the slower rhythm of the small town. Hence her need for some extra physical activity...

A sugary treat, she knew, would defeat the purpose, but she wasn't willing to sacrifice all just yet. Besides, the long walk really had left her deflated and in need of an energy boost.

"Don't you have anything to say?" Eve asked. "What's the point of bringing you along if I'm going to talk to myself?" She set her menu down. "Jill?"

"Sorry, I got caught up in the collective silence."

"The what?" Eve looked around them. The Chin Wag Café was filled to capacity doing its usual mid-morning roaring trade. It was always as busy as a bee's hive with conversation buzzing...

Eve's eyes narrowed.

Everyone had fallen silent.

"What's going on?" She turned back to Jill who'd dipped her head behind the menu. "Jill?"

Grumbling lightly, Jill emerged from behind the menu and leaned forward. "Dead on your feet?" she whispered.

"Well, yes. Working as a chef, I've spent years on my feet. There's nothing wrong with my stamina, but honestly, I must have stepped on every single loose pebble along the way from Mira's house into town."

Jill's eyebrows curved upward. "Dead on your feet," she repeated.

"Okay. You're being blatantly obvious about something. What am I missing?"

Jill huffed out a breath. "The last time you talked about death, or murder or... killing... do I need to say more?"

Eve frowned. "Are you suggesting my choice of words had something to do with inviting a killer to the island?" It had been over two months since the unfortunate incident, which had resulted in the untimely death—

Her eyes connected with Jill's. Eve slumped back in her seat and glowered at her.

"What?" Jill asked.

"You've made me self-aware."

"Were you thinking about killing, death... murder?" Jill asked.

"You brought it up. My mind was on my sore feet and what I could eat to replenish my strength. The thought of having to trek back to Mira's on foot made me think this island needs a taxi service. But that was only a fleeting thought because now I'm thinking about..." she flapped her hands, "See what you've done? Now it's all I can think about." She scooped in a big breath. "All right. From now on, I will avoid all use of that word and all derivatives associated with it. Happy now?"

"You'll burst," Jill warned. "I give you an hour and

I'm being generous."

"It's just a word."

"If you say so, but when it comes out of your mouth, it seems to gather momentum."

"You're being ridiculous and far too pedantic in your observations. You'll be the—" death of me, she finished silently.

"Yes?"

"I can do this. I can."

"Would you like to make it interesting?"

"A hundred dollars if I slip up," Eve suggested.

"A hundred? That's a bit steep."

"It shows how serious I am. I can go an hour without mentioning anything related to—"

"Yes?"

"You know very well what I'm referring to. And don't try to trip me up."

"Ready to order?" the waitress asked as she gave their table a brisk tidy up.

Eve hadn't seen her around before. She and Jill had become regulars at the café and Eve had made a point of being on first name terms with the staff. She looked at the girl's name tag.

Di.

Eve slanted her gaze toward Jill in time to see her friend trying to stifle her laughter.

She could do this. Eve gave herself a mental nudge

and told herself to avoid all mention of that which she wouldn't even think about... or any words associated with it...

"I haven't decided yet," Eve said, "Perhaps you can help me. What can you recommend as a sure-fire pick me up decadent treat?"

"Death by Chocolate Fudge Tart," Di said.

Jill chuckled.

"Can we have another moment to decide, please?" Eve leaned forward and lowering her voice, said, "How far does this moratorium on anything associated with that which I won't mention because it'll cost me a hundred dollars go?"

"Don't mind me. Do and say as you please. I could do with an extra hundred dollars." Jill shrugged. "I'll have the blueberry pancakes and a double shot espresso, please."

Eve drew in a big breath and looked up at the waitress who'd already returned to take their orders. "I'll go with your recommendation and a double shot espresso too, please."

"Double shot espresso," Di wrote, "And...?"

"The tart you recommended."

"Which one?" Di asked, "I've just served two customers and they asked for recommendations too."

"I'd like the tart you recommended to me."

The waitress raised her shoulders.

Eve slanted her gaze at Jill who was pretending to be distracted by the pattern on the tablecloth. "Do you have the tarts listed on a board somewhere so I can point to the one I want? I don't see it anywhere on the menu."

"That's because it falls under the day's specials."

"Great, so you must have a specials' board."

"No, but I'll suggest it to the owner."

"Go ahead and order it," Jill said, her eyes sparkling with mischief.

Eve bit the edge of her lip. "May I?" She gestured to the waitress's order pad. "I'll write it down for you."

"If you can write it down, why not just tell me?" the waitress asked.

"It's the chocolate tart."

"We have several of those. Which one did you want?"

Eve threw her hands up in the air. "It's the Death by Chocolate Fudge Tart, all right. There, I said it."

"That was a quick hundred dollars. And I swear that was the sound of a second death knell," Jill murmured.

"Don't be so morbid. I'm going to change the subject and there'll be no more mention of... you know what." She drummed her fingers on the table trying to come up with something else to say.

She'd met Jill soon after arriving on the island to visit her aunt Mira who'd been away at the time, and they'd since become accustomed to each other's company. In fact, not a day went by when they didn't see each other or talk on the phone.

Jill was ten years younger than her but quite mature for twenty-four. Something they had in common. At her age, Eve had been doing double shifts at a couple of restaurants trying to work her way up the ladder and get ahead in the competitive cutthroat world where men seemed to excel and get ahead far quicker than women.

"How's your painting going?" Eve rarely asked because she got to see her work-in-progress on a fairly regular basis as the house Jill shared with her parents was only a short walk away from Mira's beach house.

"I'm thinking of tackling something bigger than the usual picture postcard size."

"I like small pictures," Eve said, "There's something intimate about the size. They can still make quite a statement. You know the Mona Lisa is ridiculously small. And then there's that Dutch artist... What's his name? He painted mostly small pictures. There was a film made based on a book written about him." She clicked her fingers. "Vermeer."

"Oh, yes. *The Girl With the Pearl Earring.*"

Eve nodded. "Maybe I should open a gallery in town. Then I could display your work." She'd come to the island to spend some time redefining herself. The restaurant she'd owned with her then husband had suffered a near death—

Eve sprung upright in her chair and focused on navigating her way around any mention of death and killing and murder...

She gave a firm nod and tugged her train of thought in another direction. She'd exhausted herself, revamping the business her ex had nearly sent bankrupt. She'd since sold it and had turned her back on the food industry. She hadn't exactly made a killing—

Eve pushed out a breath.

"What's wrong? Your face's gone all red," Jill said.

Eve fanned herself with the menu. "I'm thinking it's time I come up with a plan of action. I have some thinking time money, but I don't want to wait until my funds dwindle away."

"Why don't you work in Mira's bookstore?"

Eve had already considered that. Mira had purchased Tinkerbelle's Bookstore as an investment but the existing staff knew the business inside out. She'd have nothing to contribute. "I don't know anything about books."

"What's there to know?"

"What's hot, what's new." Eve lifted her shoulder. "You know I'm not a big reader."

Jill gave her a puzzled look. "There are days when I have to force myself to put a book down and get on with my painting, and that's something else I can't go a day without doing."

Eve played with the salt and pepper shakers. "Customers would expect me to know what I'm talking about. They'd want my expert opinion." Eve waved the idea away. "I'm not a complete philistine. I've made some headway with Mira's books. In fact, I just finished reading her latest manuscript." But only because Mira had said she wanted to base the swashbuckling hero on Detective Jack Bradford and Eve had been curious to see how he'd come across on the printed page.

She hadn't been disappointed.

"Are you experiencing some sort of early menopause?" Jill asked, "Your face flushed a deep shade of crimson again."

"Don't be ridiculous. Thirty-four year olds don't get hot flushes." Eve poured herself some water and drank deeply. "The more I think about it, the more curious I am about a gallery. I already like your paintings, so I shouldn't have any trouble promoting them."

"So, you'll be comfortable if a customer makes a reference to Andrew Wyeth."

"Who's he?"

"One of my favorite artists. I have a poster of one of his paintings in my studio."

"Oh yes, he does those figures and landscapes. Very atmospheric... which is what you do in your landscapes."

"I'm impressed."

"Who else do you like?"

"Reginald Bryant Burns."

"He sounds stuffy."

"He's a recluse. Actually, he lives right here on the island."

Eve gave a pensive nod. "Now that I think about it, the name sounds familiar."

"He lives at the end of Old Coach Road."

"That's where the lighthouse is."

"That's the one. He bought it a few years ago."

"I used to hide out there when I was kid." Waiting for Frank Parkmore to go on one of his walks so she could sneak in and steal his roses to give to Mira. Eve fell silent and thought about Frank ending his days in a convalescing home after his stroke. Mira had visited him several times and had said his memory had gone. Just as well, Eve thought. It wouldn't be pleasant to think about the killer who'd been at large—

"I'd give anything to see his studio," Jill said.

"Hang on, I have heard of him." She tapped her chin trying to remember the details. "It was a newspaper article. Something about him making a killing—" Eve looked away. "How long does it take to make a cup of coffee and serve a piece of tart? I'm famished."

Jill laughed under her breath. "Those death knells are coming hard and fast."

Eve racked her brain trying to remember what she'd

read. Something about him selling a drawing. "That's right. He sold a Picasso drawing. It was nothing but a scrap of paper and he got a mint for it. His grandfather had acquired it before Picasso had made a name for himself. Rumor has it, he has another drawing stashed away."

"He comes in here at about this time every day to get coffee right after he gets his donuts from next door."

They both looked up at the waitress.

"Sorry, I overheard you mentioning Reginald Bryant Burns."

"Thank you for the heads up." Eve turned to Jill. "This is exciting. Looks like you'll get your wish after all."

Jill shrunk back into her chair. "Wish?"

"You said you'd kill—"

"Yes?"

"You said you'd give anything to see his studio. When he comes in, we can ask him for a tour."

"So which part of recluse didn't you get?"

"He's an artist. He'll be delighted to show us around. Artists are full of themselves and always out to get attention."

Jill sighed. "He's one of the top guns in the art world, not a street artist peddling his wares. He's repre-sented by one of the most prestigious art galleries in New York and has showings all over the world. The island is the one place where he can get away from it all, he said so in an interview."

Eve shook her head. "It would be a nice neighborly gesture. I bet he'll make an exception for us."

An hour and a half later, Eve caught the waitress's attention. "Another two coffees, please, Di."

Jill chuckled and rubbed her hands in glee. "Not for me, thanks. I should go. Mischief and Mr. Magoo will be pacing by now. If they don't get their midday walk, they'll be restless in the afternoon."

"It won't kill you to wait another half hour—"

Jill laughed. "That's four hundred dollars you owe me."

End of preview

Other Cozy Mystery books by Sonia Parin

A Deadline Cozy Mystery series

Sunny Side Up

Snuffed Out

All Tied Up

The Last Bite

Final Cut

Sleeping With the Fishes

A Kink in the Road

The Merry Widow

Dying Trade

A Dear Abby Cozy Mystery Series

End of the Lane

Be Still My Heart

The Last Ride

The Last Stop

The Last Dance

An Evie Parker Mystery (1920s Historical Cozy Mystery series)

House Party Murder Rap

Murder at the Tea Party

Murder at the Car Rally

Murder in the Cards

Murder at the Seaside Hotel

A Mackenzie Coven Mystery series

Witch Indeed

Witch Cast

Witch Charm

Witch Trials

A Mackenzie Coven Collection

Witch in Exile

Witch Namaste - A Mackenzie Coven Mystery Short

Good Witch Hunting - A Mackenzie Coven Mystery Short

'Tis the Season to be Creepy - A Mackenzie Coven Mystery Short

Good Witch Hunting - A Mackenzie Coven Mystery Short

Potion Heist - A Mackenzie Coven Mystery Short

The Power of Two and a Half - A Mackenzie Coven
Mystery Short
Witch Fairy Tale

Made in the USA
Columbia, SC
24 May 2020

98164659R00121